An Unforgivable Secret

AMISH SECRETS
~ BOOK 1 ~

J. E. B. Spredemann

Blessed Publishing

BOOKS BY J.E.B. SPREDEMANN

Available Now:

AMISH GIRLS SERIES (for teens)

Joanna's Struggle

Danika's Journey

Chloe's Revelation

Susanna's Surprise

Annie's Decision

NOVELLAS

Amish by Accident*

An Unforgivable Secret*(AMISH SECRETS SERIES)

Coming Soon:

AMISH GIRLS SERIES

Abigail's Triumph – fall 2013

Brooke's Quest – winter 2013

Leah's Legacy (Amish Girls Series - Book 8) – February 2014

NOVELLAS

A Secret Encounter *(AMISH SECRETS SERIES) – winter 2013

Learning to Love – Saul's Story* – 2014

To everyone who has had to use Plan B

Author's Note

It should be noted that the Amish people and their communities differ one from another. There are, in fact, no two Amish communities exactly alike. It is this premise on which this book is written. We have taken cautious steps to assure the authenticity of Amish practices and customs. Both Old Order Amish and New Order Amish are portrayed in this work of fiction and may be inconsistent with some Amish communities.

We, as *Englischers,* can learn a lot from the Plain People and their simple way of life. Their hard work, close-knit family life, and concern for others are to be applauded. As the Lord wills, may this special culture continue to be respected and remain so for many centuries to come, and may God's light of salvation reach their hearts.

Characters in An Unforgivable Secret

Hannah Stolzfus – Protagonist, Christian's *aldi* (sweetheart)

Deborah Stolzfus – Hannah's younger sister

Miriam Stolzfus – Hannah's mother

Silas Stolzfus – Hannah's father

Christian Glick – Hannah's beau

Samuel Beachy – Christian's best friend, also a friend of Hannah

Peter Beachy – Samuel's younger brother, Deborah's beau

Paul Beachy – Samuel's father

Timothy Beachy – Samuel's uncle in Ohio

Carolanne – Samuel's long-distance *aldi*

Judah Hostettler – Bishop of Paradise Amish church district

Jonathan Fisher – Minister

Chloe – Midwife, Protagonist of Chloe's Revelation

Danika Yoder – Herb doctor, Protagonist of Danika's Journey

Joanna Scott – Jonathan's older sister, Protagonist of Joanna's Struggle

Caleb Scott – Joanna's husband, missionary

Julia – Teen from out-of-state Amish district

Kristine – *Englisch* girl

Unofficial Glossary
of Pennsylvania Dutch Words

Ab im kopp – Crazy

Ach – Oh

Ausbund – Amish hymn book

Bloobier – Blueberry

Boppli – Baby

Bopplin – Babies

Bruder – Brother

Dat, Daed – Dad

Dawdi – Grandfather

Demut – Humility

Denki – Thanks

Der Herr – The Lord

Dochder – Daughter

Dokter – Doctor

Dummkopp – Dummy

Englischer – A non-Amish person

Ferhoodled – Mixed up, Crazy

Fraa – Woman, Wife

Gern gheschen – You're welcome

Gott – God

Grank – Sick, ill

Grossboppli – Grandbaby

Gross Dawdi – Great Grandfather

Gut – Good

Guten mayrie – Good morning

Guten nacht – Good night

Haus – House

Hiya – Hi

Hochmut – Pride

Hullo – Hello

Ich liebe dich – I love you

Jah – Yes

Kapp – Prayer Covering

Kinskinner – Grandchildren

Kumm – Come

Lieb – Love

Liede – Song

Mamm – Mom

Mammi – Grandmother

Mei Lieb – My Love

Mein Liewe – My Dear

Mudder – Mother

Nee – No

Ordnung – Rules of the Amish community

Rumspringa – Running around years

Schatzi – Honey

Schweschder – Sister

Vadder – Father

Verboten – Forbidden

Vorsinger – Song leader

Wilkom – Welcome

Wunderbaar – Wonderful

PROLOGUE

It is a secret I intend to keep buried forever. But like all secrets, it begs to be told. Nobody knows. Only me. And if I had my way, not even I would know. The secret is powerful. It has the potential to destroy my life. On the other hand, if revealed, could it possibly bring a sense of peace to my soul? But I will never tell a soul. Ever.

ONE

*E*xhausted, Hannah Stolzfus clambered down from the buggy. *Dat* met her at the barn and led Winnie to the water trough. "Another busy day at the candle shop?" *Dat's* bushy eyebrows rose.

"*Jah, Dat.* Lots of *Englischers* today. I guess the *kinner* are out of school now that it's summertime and it seems lots of folks are visiting Lancaster for their holiday this year," Hannah said.

"It wonders me why the *Englisch* find our ways so interesting." Silas Stolzfus stroked his beard with his thumb and forefinger.

"I think maybe they want to be like us. I saw another new book at Yoder's Market yesterday. It had a woman on the cover with a *kapp*, but the hair was all wrong. Looked pretty funny to me. *Ach*, I can't imagine what *Mamm* would say if I cut my hair short across the front like the *Englisch*."

"If they want to be like us, why don't they give up their fancy cars and their *electric*?" *Dat* added, "*Nee*, I'm afraid it would be difficult giving up something you've known your whole life. I, for one, would not want to give up my farm."

"That's because you are a *gut* farmer and a *gut* steward of the land *Gott* has given you."

"*Demut*, Hannah. It is only by the strength *Der Herr* gives me that I can work this land." *Dat* leaned over and placed a hand on Hannah's forearm. "You are a *gut* daughter, and wise to think such things."

"If I am wise it is only because of what you and *Mamm* have taught me," Hannah deflected with a smile before making her way toward the back door of the house.

Silas released a contented sigh and grinned as he watched Hannah enter the house. Out of all four of his daughters, she was certainly the most well-grounded and levelheaded. His youngest daughter, on the other hand, was quite a different story. He knew how often Deborah sneaked out of the house at night but was glad that she often roped Hannah into going with her. He got the feeling Hannah only went to keep her sister from dabbling in too much mischief.

"Hannah," Deborah whispered, shaking her sister's shoulder. "Hannah, wake up."

Groggily, Hannah turned over on her side. "What is it, Deborah?" Hannah groaned.

"Leah can't go with me tonight. You have to come. I told Peter I would meet him at the movie theater. Leah's beau canceled and now she doesn't want to go," Deborah said pouting.

"I'm tired, Deb. We had customers non-stop today and I barely had enough time to complete my chores before bed," Hannah reasoned.

Deborah rolled her eyes. "Hannah, you're eighteen years old and you're acting like *Mammi*."

"I am not," Hannah snapped back. "And if you had a mind to get yourself a job, you might find yourself a little tired too. Instead you do everything you can to get out of work."

"I do not. I'm in my *rumspringa*. I've got a right to have a little fun," Deborah said, pulling up a pair of jeans under her dress. "Fine. If you won't go with me I'll just go by myself."

Hannah sighed and rolled out of bed. "Okay, I'll come with you but I'm not wearing *Englisch* clothes."

"If you want to be the only one in an *Englisch* movie theater dressed Plain, fine. But I aim to fit in. Besides, Peter likes it when I wear these jeans." Deb gave Hannah a sly look.

"*Ach*, did he tell ya that?" Hannah donned her *kapp* and pinned it into place.

"*Nee*, but I can tell by the way he looks at me. I'm sure Christian would look at you that way too if you dressed in *Englisch* clothes like this," Deborah said unabashedly, showing off her snug jeans and fitted shirt.

Incredulous, Hannah gasped. "I certainly don't want to attract that kind of attention from Christian. It's...it's sinful."

Deborah rolled her eyes. "*Ach*, Hannah. Have you no sense of fun?"

"It's that sense of fun that lands girls in trouble," Hannah insisted.

"Come on Plain Jane, let's go now."

Hannah shook her head in disbelief and reluctantly followed her impervious sister out the door.

Hannah stood at the back of the movie theater auditorium waiting for her eyes to adjust. Deborah and Peter had already found their seats, but Hannah had no clue where they were. She had decided using the restroom before the movie started would be good idea, but had to wait in a long line. By the time she entered the theater, the previews had already begun. *It's nearly impossible to see anything in here*, Hannah thought, squinting. After giving up locating her sister, she sat down in the back row alone.

Samuel Beachy entered the movie theater a little late. After his friend Christian ditched him for dinner with an *Englisch* girl, he figured he didn't want to spend the evening bored to death. The movie theater was the only other thing open on this side of town at this late hour. Fortunately, the movie that looked most interesting had just begun and he could slip in before the previews were over. He normally didn't care to watch *Englisch* movies, but figured it was better than the alternative.

As he looked around for a good seat, he noticed an Amish girl in the back row. Due to the darkness, he couldn't tell if it was someone from his district or not. He approached the row and walked near to where the young woman sat. A bright flash from the movie screen illuminated her face and he realized it was Hannah Stolzfus, Christian's *aldi.*

What is she doing here alone? He wondered. He was glad Christian and the *Englisch* girl hadn't come here. If so, Hannah was sure to be disheartened seeing her beau with another girl. Samuel determined he would keep her company.

"*Hiya,*" he whispered.

"*Ach, hullo,* Samuel." Hannah's face brightened as she looked past him. "Is Christian with you?"

Samuel grimaced inwardly. "*Nee.* I'm here alone. Do you mind if I join ya?"

Hannah shrugged. "I guess that would be all right." She decided. "I'm here with my *schweschder* and her beau – your *bruder.*"

Samuel looked around the large darkened auditorium, but the young couple was nowhere in sight. He leaned over and whispered, "Hey, want some popcorn?"

Hannah hesitated. "But it's so expensive."

"My treat. It won't break me, I promise." He winked.

"Sure." She smiled, thinking the popcorn smelled good. She wouldn't have wasted money buying her own at an exorbitant amount when she could make it at home for just pennies, but Samuel seemed eager to purchase some.

"I'll be right back." Samuel disappeared for a few minutes, and then promptly returned with a large tub of popcorn. He offered her some and she happily took a large handful of the buttery goodness and popped some into her mouth. "*Ach*, it's a *gut* thing I got the big one," he teased.

"You mean I gotta share it with you?" She grinned.

"Yes, but these are all yours," he said, handing her a box of chocolate malt balls and a bottle of water.

"*Ach*, Samuel. *Denki*." Hannah couldn't believe Samuel's generosity; he'd always been kind-hearted. She was thankful that Christian had such a *gut* friend.

Samuel delighted in seeing Hannah's face light up. Christian had found a good woman; it was a shame he wasn't treating her the way she deserved. The three of them had grown up together and had always been *gut* friends. It seemed that Hannah had blossomed from an awkward tomboy into a beautiful young lady overnight. Unfortunately, both Samuel and Christian had noticed at the same time. The very night Samuel had in mind to ask Hannah if he could take her home from a singing was the night she rode in Christian's buggy for the first time. That was over a year ago. Since then, Samuel had respected them as a couple and kept his distance from Hannah.

Meanwhile, last fall Samuel had met Carolanne. He had moved to Ohio for a few months to help out with his uncle's corn harvest. After he had taken Carolanne home from a few singings, he'd asked her to be his *aldi*. When he returned to Pennsylvania, they continued their long-distance relationship by writing letters to each other at least once a month. He planned on returning to Ohio one day to make Carolanne his bride when he was certain she was the one. But he just wasn't certain.

What would happen to Hannah if things didn't work out between her and Christian? Would she give Samuel a chance? As Samuel sat next to Hannah, watching her watch the movie, he was tempted to take her hand. But he wouldn't. Surely she would be put off by it. Sitting here with her almost felt like a date; if only it was.

As the movie progressed, Hannah could hardly keep her eyelids open. It seemed like only a few minutes had gone by when she felt a gentle patting on her arm. She woke up to find herself leaning against Samuel. He slipped his arm from around her shoulder when she became fully coherent.

"*Ach*, I'm sorry, Samuel," Hannah said, feeling like a *dummkopp.*

"*Nee*, it's okay. Fall asleep on me anytime." He smiled. "Perhaps you should try to find your *schweschder* now."

Hannah arose from her seat yawning and stretched long and wide. Although her catnap was short, she felt rejuvenated for the drive home. As the lights turned back on, Hannah scanned the audience in search of her sister and Peter. It would've been much easier to spot her sister if she'd dressed Plain.

She heard a buzz emanating from Samuel's pocket and he retrieved his cell phone, indicating to her he was going to step out into the lobby. Normally, the Amish in their district didn't use cell phones, but Samuel had been granted permission to own one for his buggy making business.

Since most of the young people her age were in *rumspringa*, many of them did own cell phones. Although they didn't approve of it, the leaders turned a blind eye to their usage because they realized *rumspringa* was an important time in a young person's life. It was a time when they would choose the course of their lives and the leaders didn't want to hinder their decision making. Of course, they still advocated holiness and blatant rebellion was never accepted. After all, each one would have to give their own account to God.

Hannah found Deborah and Peter near the front of the auditorium and quickly made her way to them before they disappeared.

"Hannah, Peter's going to take me home," Deborah stated matter-of-factly. "You don't mind taking the buggy by yourself, do you?" Deborah's eyes pleaded.

Hannah sighed. She didn't relish driving the buggy alone at night, but she wouldn't begrudge her sister's request. Hannah knew time alone with a beau was few and far between, and she often coveted more time with Christian. She nodded and gave Deb the 'you'd better stay out of trouble' look.

Deborah squealed and hugged her sister. "*Denki*, Hannah."

Hannah made her way out to the lobby with purse in hand and searched for Samuel to say goodbye, but he was nowhere to be seen. After she exited the large glass doors, she found the buggy in the parking lot. Thankfully the lot was well lit, because she didn't care to be alone in a public place after dark. She stroked Winnie's coat a few times before ascending the buggy. Somehow, having a horse with her gave her a semblance of companionship and security.

"Hannah!" She heard Samuel's voice call out as he sprinted toward her. Hannah turned to his attention as he neared the buggy. "Do you mind if I catch a ride with ya? My ride left without me," he explained.

"Only if you agree to drive," she said smiling.

"Deal," he agreed.

Hannah moved over and handed the reins to Samuel. "I'm glad you're here. I don't care to drive alone in the dark."

"And I'm glad you're here because I don't like to walk home alone in the dark," he said setting the horse in motion.

Hannah laughed. "I reckon you were worse off than I was. It's too bad your *Englisch* friends left you all alone." Hannah knew Samuel and Christian had *Englisch* friends they sometimes hung out with. In fact, many of the Plain people had *Englisch* friends. But she knew Christian would be at home sleeping after working hard in the field all day.

If only that were the case, Samuel thought. He moved the buggy out onto the main road now, heading toward their small rural community. "Are ya goin' to the gathering tomorrow night?" Samuel asked.

"*Jah*. Me and Christian are," she said.

Samuel sighed. *Hannah is so trusting. Doesn't Christian realize what he's doing? She is such a wonderful girl.* Samuel hated to see Hannah get her heart broken, but he felt it wasn't his place to say anything about Christian's unfaithfulness. He would bide his time in silence.

"Are ya still writing to Carolanne?" she asked.

"*Jah.*" Although, at this moment he felt his heart was betraying her.

"How is it out in Ohio? Is it as beautiful as Lancaster County?" she wondered aloud.

"It's nice," he said eying Hannah up and down out of the corner of his eye. "But not near as beautiful." Yep, he was definitely betraying her. *You are a hypocrite, Samuel Beachy. How can you bemoan Christian's unfaithfulness to Hannah when your own thoughts are betraying Carolanne?* Samuel shook off his conscience. *Carolanne is not betrothed to me.*

"*Denki* for the ride, Samuel. And your company at the movie theater," Hannah offered, as they neared her property.

The pleasure is all mine. "*Gern Gheschen.* I'll just unhitch the buggy and put Winnie up, then walk home. You may go inside already if you'd like. I know you're tired."

"All right. *Guten nacht*, Samuel."

Samuel watched as Hannah safely entered her quiet home. *Too bad I never had a chance with her.* Nonetheless, he would look forward to seeing her tomorrow night. Even if she was sitting next to his unworthy best friend.

TWO

Christian Glick contemplated the young folks gathering he and Hannah would be attending tonight. He enjoyed spending time with his friends in his Amish community, but also liked hanging out with his *Englisch* friends. He thought about Kristine, the *Englisch* girl he'd seen a few times. She was cute with her curly short blonde hair and turned up nose. Not to mention her figure that he couldn't help but notice when she wore her tight jeans and low-cut blouse.

If Hannah ever found out... he wouldn't think about that now. He and Samuel were the only ones in their Plain community that he knew of, who knew about Kristine. And he completely trusted his best friend Samuel. They had been good friends since their school days and there was no one who knew Samuel better than he did. He knew he would eventually have to cut Kristine off when he got baptized into the church in the fall, but he was enjoying his last few days of *rumspringa.* He also knew he'd never marry a girl like Kristine. She would never be the kind of wife he desired. No, Hannah was the one for him.

Christian's conscience did prick him, though, when he was with Hannah. The two girls were so different. Kristine was bubbly and excitable, while Hannah was more down-to-earth and thoughtful. He wished that he could somehow have both of them wrapped up into one, but he couldn't. Because he planned to remain Amish all his days, he decided Hannah would be the best choice for a mate.

But for some reason, he couldn't get the kisses out of his mind that he and Kristine had shared in the back seat of her car last night. He and Hannah had kissed before too, but she definitely wasn't as willing as Kristine was. *Perhaps that's why our leaders are always warning us about courting so many different girls. It seems like I'm always comparing Hannah and Kristine to each other and I know it isn't fair to either of them. I need to tell Kristine goodbye next time I see her,* he decided. *But tonight, I'm going to ask Hannah to marry me.*

Hannah knew Christian would be in her driveway any minute. She had taken extra care to pin up her hair just so, and was sure to wear Christian's favorite dress that brought out the green in her hazel eyes. She pinched her cheeks to add a little color to her face and sprayed on a bit of wildflower perfume.

"Your *kapp* is crooked," Miriam Stolzfus called from the door, smiling.

Hannah startled. "*Ach, Mamm.* I didn't know you were there."

"Christian will think you look just fine."

Hannah's eyes widened and her mouth hung open. "*Ach,* how did you know Christian Glick was courtin' me?"

"I have eyes, don't I?" *Mamm* said.

"Is it that obvious?"

"It's nearly impossible to miss the look of love. I've seen your eyes wander his way more than once." Miriam neared and helped Hannah secure her *kapp* into place. "You know, your *dat* and I will miss you when you're gone."

"*Ach, Mamm.* Christian hasn't even asked me yet," Hannah said.

"No, but I'm certain he will. He'd be a foolish man to let a girl like you get away. And I know Christian Glick is no fool."

Deborah's voice called from the stairs, "Hannah, you-know-who is waiting at the end of the lane for you."

"I gotta go, *Mamm. Denki* for everything." Hannah leaned over and kissed her mother's cheek, something she didn't do often but felt was appropriate at present.

She hurried out the door and calmly walked, like a respectable Amish woman should, to Christian's carriage. Christian leaned over and held out his hand to assist her entrance into the buggy.

"How's my favorite *maedel* doing?" Christian's gorgeous blue eyes sparkled. Truthfully, it peeved Hannah when he spoke like that. It sounded as though he had more than one *aldi.* But she knew he was only teasing, so she just smiled.

"Fine. And how are you?" she asked.

"Better than ever now that you're by my side," Christian charmed.

"You're *ferhoodled*," Hannah said laughingly.

"*Nee*. Just *ab im kopp* over you." Christian took her hand to his lips and kissed it.

"*Ach*, Christian we're in broad daylight. Anyone can see," she protested. "Besides, I think you'd better pay attention to the road."

"Don't worry, *Lieb*. Cowboy knows the way to the Yoders'," Christian said confidently. "And I don't care who sees. Everyone will soon know how much you mean to me."

Hannah gave him a sideways glance. *What did he mean by that?* "You really *are* acting strange."

"Maybe I'm just excited that you're going to say yes to what I'm going to ask you."

"What if I say no?" Hannah asked defiantly, still clueless as to what they were talking about.

"You really don't want to get hitched?" Christian's previous excitement deflated.

"What? *Hitched*?" Hannah asked in surprise. "Christian Glick, are you asking me to marry you?"

"*Jah*, that's what I was going to ask," he said quietly.

"Yes. I'll marry you," she answered calmly.

Christian guided Cowboy off the road and brought the rig to a stop. He leaned over and kissed Hannah full on the lips. "*Denki*, Hannah," he said excitedly. "You won't be sorry. And I know you'll make a *wunderbaar fraa* too. We'll have lots of *kinner*." He passionately kissed her again and she gently pushed him away.

"Yes, Christian, but the *kinner* have to come *later*," she emphasized.

"Uh, *jah*, right." Christian sheepishly scooted back to his side of the buggy seat, but his eyes sparkled with joy.

Samuel noticed that Hannah and Christian were beaming as they entered the young folks gathering in the Yoders' barn. As soon as he was able to catch Christian's attention, he signaled him outside for a chat. Reluctantly, Christian left Hannah's side and joined him behind the barn.

"What's going on, Christian?" Samuel asked coolly.

"I asked Hannah to marry me and she said yes," he said quietly so nobody but Samuel could hear.

"Are you crazy?" Samuel hissed disgustedly.

"What do mean? Don't you think she's a great girl?" Christian played dumb.

"That's not what I'm talking about and you know it," Samuel said, looking around to be sure no one else was nearby to eavesdrop on their conversation. He lowered his voice and looked intently at Christian. "What about the *Englisch* girl? You know, the one you ditched me for last night?"

"Oh yeah, sorry about that. I see you found a way home," Christian said nonchalantly. "Don't worry about Kristine, I'll drop her next Friday."

Exasperated, Samuel found controlling his volume difficult. "I can't believe you. You're betrothed to an Amish girl and you have a date with an *Englisch* girl on Friday? Don't you think you're doin' things in the wrong order?"

"Back off, Samuel. It's nobody's business but mine. And no one knows about that except you and me. And that's the way we're going to keep it. Right?"

"You're not being fair to Hannah," Samuel insisted.

"I told you that I'm breaking things off with the *Englisch* girl," Christian spewed.

"Fine. I won't say anything," he spat back. "But if you don't end it Friday –"

"I said I would," Christian said curtly before stomping off. He couldn't go back into the barn now. Hannah would see his frustrated countenance and know something was wrong. He needed to take a walk to cool down and gather his wits about him. Why did Samuel care so much anyway?

"So, is it true?" Deborah whispered across the room to Hannah as they lay awake in bed that night.

"What?"

"Okay, I'll spell it out for you." She rolled her eyes. "Did Christian really ask you to marry him?"

"Where did you hear that?" Hannah wondered aloud.

"Answer my question first," Deborah insisted.

"Deb, you know these things are supposed to be kept secret."

"Well?"

"*Jah.* But you better not tell anybody."

Deborah squealed, "He did? For real?"

Hannah nodded, unsure if Deborah could even see her in the dark.

"I thought so. That's so romantic! What did he say?"

"I'm not going to tell you!"

"I wonder what happened between Christian and Samuel at the gathering," Deborah commented, changing the subject.

"I'm sure it's none of your business."

"So, you don't know? You didn't even ask Christian why Samuel left early?"

"It's none of my business either," Hannah insisted.

"Sally said she heard them arguing outside Yoders' barn. She thought it was about you," Deborah said.

"That's enough, Deb. What happens between Samuel and Christian is their business and nobody else's."

"Aren't you at all curious?"

"No, now go to sleep. I've got to get up early tomorrow." Hannah rolled over and pulled the sheet up over her shoulders, kicking off the heavy quilt. As she drifted off to sleep, though, she did wonder what had transpired between Christian and Samuel. Surely it wasn't about her.

THREE

Hannah scanned the occupants of the crowded restaurant. Their brightly-colored clothing seemed to mesh with the fifties décor that adorned the otherwise plain walls. Yep, once again, she was the only plainly-dressed person in the dining room. Of course, what respectable Amish person would be out at this hour anyway? Certainly not her, if she didn't feel it was necessary to tag along with her sister. Why couldn't Deborah just see her beau at the Amish gatherings and singings they attended?

They seemed to be sufficient for her and Christian. And now she was betrothed to her handsome beau! At first, she'd been a little surprised that Christian had asked. After all, they'd barely been courting for a year now. But she gladly said yes in anticipation of fulfilling all of her childhood dreams. She'd once read a storybook in the waiting room at the dentist's office. *Mamm* had been busy with little Deborah at the time so she didn't realize Hannah had sneaked over to the basket of books in the corner. She read all about a princess that longed to find the man of her dreams, her perfect prince. She just knew that one day a nice Amish boy, who was head-over-heels for her, would one day sweep her off her feet and they'd live happily ever after. And she'd finally found the one.

While she haphazardly perused the menu for the third time, she finally decided on a bowl of fruit and a small salad. She did not need to add on any extra pounds, especially in light of her upcoming wedding. As she studied a poster of a person called Elvis on the wall, pondering why he wore such a funny hair-do, more patrons came pouring in. Although the restaurant seemed to portray a bygone era, customers enjoyed the atmosphere. Hannah's main gripe was the *Englischers'* songs that seemed to get stuck in her head. It wouldn't be so bad if she didn't like them, but the love songs seemed to have a lasting effect causing her heart to flip-flop when she heard them. They just made her long for her wedding day even more.

"Deb, I don't know why you and Peter insist on seeing each other every free moment you get," Hannah complained when Peter had gotten up to ask for a refill of their ketchup bottle.

"That's because we're still in love. The flame hasn't died out like it has with you and Christian," Deborah teased.

"Christian and I are getting along just fine and you know it," Hannah insisted.

Deborah suddenly shielded her face. "Oh my...don't look now, Hannah," Deborah warned. "But Christian is here with *Englisch* friends."

"What?" Hannah couldn't help but turn around after hearing that.

Sure enough, there was Christian dressed in *Englisch* clothes. His hair was combed differently, similar to the *Englisch* styles of some of the other young men in the restaurant. She had to admit he looked handsome as an *Englischer*. She quickly turned back around and placed a hand over her rapidly-beating heart.

What is Christian doing here? Discreetly, she turned around to look at the corner booth on the opposite side of the restaurant where he sat with three other *Englisch* dressed young people – another guy and two girls. Christian sat next to an immodestly dressed girl and...*he's holding her hand?* Hannah heard Christian's hearty laugh carry across the noisy restaurant and he leaned over and kissed the *Englisch* girl on the lips. *Oh no, this cannot be happening!*

Tears filled Hannah's eyes. "Deb, I want to go home now."

Deborah looked back over to the booth to see what was going on. "Oh Hannah, I'm so sorry. Okay, let's go. I'll tell Peter we need to leave. We'll slip out so Christian doesn't see," Deborah said cooperatively. She hurried to the bar stools where Peter stood patiently waiting for the ketchup and quickly whispered something in his ear. He glanced over Deb's shoulder at Hannah and nodded, then pecked Deborah on the cheek, causing her to blush. Peter had never been so forward in public. Perhaps it was his way of giving Deb his reassurance.

After a hasty exit from the restaurant, Hannah and Deborah set for home at a steady trot. "*Ach*, Hannah. What are you going to do?" Deb asked.

Hannah brushed away a fresh wave of tears with shaky hands. "I don't know. I had no idea. Why would he ask me to marry him if he was seeing an *Englisch* girl?"

"I don't know."

"I can't go to the singing now."

"Oh yes you can and you will, Hannah Stolzfus! You are not going to let that...that *dummkopp* ruin your life. You are going to go to the singing and let him have a piece of your mind," Deborah stated forcefully.

"*Nee*...I couldn't do that," Hannah replied to her strong-willed sister.

"Well, if you won't then I will!"

"This doesn't concern you, Deb. Please don't say anything. I...I will talk to Christian," she said unsurely as her stomach turned over. "Let's not talk about this anymore. I don't feel well."

Deborah wrung her hands. "All right...ugh, that good-for-nothing, two-timing –"

"Deb, please."

"Okay, then give me the reins because I need something to take my mind off that...that...man," she insisted.

Hannah sank into her bed and wept into her pillow, hoping Deborah couldn't hear her sobs in her bed across the room. Moonlight filtered in through the blinds illuminating their bedroom, but the bright glow couldn't penetrate the darkness that surrounded her heart. All of Hannah's expectations and dreams for the future had been crushed this terrible night. So many condescending thoughts had filled her mind and she couldn't help but second guess herself. *What's wrong with me? Am I too boring for him? Am I so inadequate that Christian has to have an* Englisch *girl too? I must not be pretty enough. And I know my body could never compete with the* Englisch *girl's perfect figure. Why, God? What did I do wrong?*

Tomorrow she would find out. She didn't know what she would say to Christian or how she'd confront him, but it had to be done.

FOUR

Christian entered the Schrock's barn wondering why Hannah hadn't come with him tonight. He'd waited at the usual spot, but after about fifteen minutes he'd given up and come alone. He'd been tempted to go up to the house and find out what the problem was but decided against it, given the hour. He hoped she wasn't sick or anything.

Although it had been difficult, he had finally broken things off with Kristine. When she asked him why, he simply told her that he was Amish and planned to remain that way. *That* was enough to scare her off. What Englisch woman would want to give up her carefree lifestyle for a rigid Amish one? None that he'd ever heard of. Of course, there was Brianna Beiler who had sort of become Amish by accident, but that was a different story. Due to a unique, somewhat rare form of amnesia, she had forgotten her previous *Englisch* life and thought she was Amish. But she hadn't known that she was ever *Englisch* in the first place.

Christian now pondered his future. It felt good to be free of Kristine, like a weight had been lifted. His heart was no longer divided now. He could give all his devotion to Hannah and get excited as they planned their wedding together. Just a few months and she'd be his completely, and boy, was he looking forward to it. Hannah would be the perfect wife.

As he and Samuel sat around talking and indulging in snacks, more young people began arriving. He informed Samuel that he'd broken up with the *Englisch* girl, and to that he just nodded. He knew Samuel had never approved of him seeing two girls at once, especially when one of them was their good friend. Samuel and Hannah had been the best friends he'd ever had, so he understood Samuel's concern.

Christian pulled out his pocket watch. Apparently, they'd come a little earlier than normal. He usually took his time when driving with Hannah, wanting to spend as many extra moments with her as possible. He caught sight of Hannah's buggy through the open barn door and his heart skipped a beat. She was so beautiful, like a pure white lily. He couldn't wait for the drive home tonight. But why had Hannah brought her own buggy? Perhaps her sister Deborah needed to use it to get home.

I don't know if I can do this, Hannah thought as she neared the barn. She did not want to break down in tears in front of everybody; she'd already done that enough at home today. She had a mind to turn around and head back to the buggy and began to do so when Deborah grasped her arm.

"*Nee,* Hannah. You have to do this. Christian needs to be confronted," Deborah insisted.

Hannah knew she was right, but it didn't make the task any easier. With dwindling confidence, she made a beeline for the snack table, hoping the distraction would calm her frayed nerves. She didn't dare look in Christian's direction although she knew he and Samuel would be in their usual spot, probably cutting up as they always did. How could Christian carry on a double life? She'd always thought he'd been sincere in his affections toward her. But she was obviously wrong.

"Hannah," Christian's familiar voice echoed behind her. She knew if she turned around they would be face to face, so she kept her back to him. "Where were you? Why didn't you ride with me tonight?"

It took every fiber in Hannah's being not to erupt into a conniption. She grimaced and clenched her fists tightly. "I thought you'd be with your *Englisch aldi,*" she replied as calmly as her voice would allow.

Christian's eyes widened. "Ha – Hannah, I..." Resigned, Christian sighed. "Let's go outside and talk."

Silently, but still not looking in Christian's direction, Hannah walked outside. As she and Christian neared the Schrock's white pasture fence, Christian took her arm and stopped her. Hannah hastily pulled her arm away. Just the thought of him touching her after seeing him holding hands with the *Englisch* girl disgusted her.

"Hannah...I – I don't know what to say. I don't know how you found out, but you must believe me when I say that I'm not seeing Kristine anymore," Christian said, wishing she'd face him.

Kristine. It was a name she would now hate for as long as she lived. She wished Christian hadn't said the name because, before a few seconds ago, she actually liked it. Not anymore. Now the name would forever be synonymous with harlot, thief, and destroyer of dreams. She knew that she was being partially irrational. In fact, the pretty *Englisch* girl probably had no idea Christian was two-timing her. She was probably just as innocent in the whole matter as Hannah was. Nevertheless, Hannah's mind wasn't thinking rationally at this moment. She was running on her emotions, which could be a dangerous thing.

Christian tentatively placed his hand on her shoulder. "Say something, Hannah."

She shrugged his hand off. "You're right, Christian. I don't believe you. The Amish man dressed in *Englisch* clothes at the restaurant last night certainly didn't act like he was about to break up with his girlfriend."

"But I did," he insisted.

Hannah spun around and looked him squarely in the eye. "You know what? I don't care, Christian. You've shown me that you are not faithful and I can't trust you." She determined not to let him see her cry.

"Hannah, you must know that I love you."

Of all the nerve! "What? You've got to be joking. If that's love, you can keep it for yourself. Or give it to your *Englischer.* I don't want any part of it."

"Hannah..." Christian hung his head. He realized he'd blown it. "Will you please just give me another chance? I want to marry you."

Exasperated, Hannah's shaky voice replied, "You want to marry me? How can you even talk of marriage now?" The tears fell from her eyes, and she was unable to stop them.

Christian attempted to pull her close, but she pushed him away. "Don't touch me!" she said.

"I'm sorry, Hannah."

"Sorry isn't enough." With that, Hannah stomped off toward the barn where voices were now lifted in song. There was no way her heart could sing now. She'd tell Deborah she was leaving, and then she would go. Hopefully, Deb didn't mind taking the buggy because Hannah needed to walk off the negative energy she emanated.

Christian gave up on reasoning with Hannah and decided to go home. He needed to come up with a plan on how he could get Hannah back. This evening definitely didn't turn out how he'd hoped.

FIVE

Monday morning, the following week...

With a gentle swaying motion, the train nearly lulled Samuel to sleep. Ohio was an hour away yet. The time had finally come, not by will, but of necessity. Hopefully Uncle Timothy wouldn't mind him showing up without prior notice. *Nee*, Samuel was certain he'd be happy to see him. He and his *dat's* youngest *bruder* had always gotten along well, probably due to their close proximity in age, and they'd bonded over the last summer when Samuel had worked side by side with him in the corn field.

Samuel thought of the letters he'd hastily written, just prior to leaving: one to his folks and the other to Christian. He'd contemplated penning one to Hannah as well, but decided against it for several reasons. Number one, he worried about it falling into the wrong hands; number two, the letter to Christian pretty much summed things up and he was certain Christian would share it with Hannah; and number three, he just didn't know what to say to her. His heart ached just thinking of her. *Ach*, she was so lovely...

Stop it, she's not yours, Samuel berated himself.

Leaving home for *gut* had been one of the hardest things he'd ever done, especially the way he'd left. But it was the only way. He was certain that if he hadn't left then and there, his relationship with Christian would not have survived. The love of a woman was not something he wished to contend for, especially when his unsuspecting adversary was also his best friend. Samuel's decision had certainly not been an easy one. He wished with all his heart that he and Hannah could be together, but not at the cost of losing Christian. He'd already crossed a forbidden boundary – one he never should have been near in the first place.

No, he could not deny that his heart desired Hannah. Sometimes, though, the heart's desire is best kept buried deep within oneself and forgotten. And that is what must happen. Christian never need know about Hannah and Samuel.

As the train car began to slow and then finally halted altogether, Samuel realized that his daydreaming had cost him his much-needed nap. Resignedly, he gathered his things and made his way toward the exit. Now he needed to hire a driver to take him to his uncle's place. He scanned the perimeter of the train depot in search of a pay phone. In his haste to leave, he'd forgotten his cell phone on his dresser at home. But maybe it was best that way. If Hannah tried to call him, he might just up and return home at the sound of her voice. No, this way was best. It had to be.

"Samuel! Samuel!" Timothy's voice called from behind him. His uncle walked toward him with purposeful strides.

"How did you know I'd be here?" Samuel wondered.

"Paul, your *dat,* called me this morn when he got your note. He figured you'd be here this afternoon sometime, so I figured I'd save you the hassle of hiring a driver. Besides, time in my buggy will give us a chance to talk about what's botherin' you," he said knowingly.

Samuel's eyebrows rose. "What do you mean by that?"

"A man doesn't just up and leave his home from one day to the next unless he's running away from something. Or someone?" Timothy asked.

Samuel sighed. "Am I that easy to read?"

Timothy chuckled. "I guess you are. Want to talk about it?"

"It was a woman," he simply said.

"Ah, that explains it."

"*Nee,* you don't understand. Christian, he's my best friend. Hannah…" Just saying her name aloud brought sorrow to Samuel's heart. "She's *his* sweetheart. But Hannah and I have gotten too close."

"Well, in that case it looks like you made the right decision. Perhaps another *maedel* will take your mind off the forbidden, *jah?* Carolanne is over today helping Mary with a quilt for the upcoming auction. I know she'll be happy to see ya. Mary tells me the two of you have been sending letters."

"*Jah.* Carolanne is a nice *maedel.*"

"She'll make a fine *fraa* for someone," Timothy said, then scratched his beard. "Ya know, there's a small farm not too far from our place – just down the road a piece. Came up for sale a few weeks ago. It's got a nice shop that would be perfect for your buggy makin'. And there ain't no buggy makers in these parts. We gotta go all the way to Bishop Burkholder's district to get our buggies. Ya got any money saved up?"

Samuel's eyebrows shot up. This was indeed *gut* news. Perhaps the Lord was paving the way for him. "*Jah*, I probably have enough for a down payment."

"*Gut. Gut.* So, ya think you'll stay?" Timothy's voice hinted of hopefulness.

"*Jah.*"

"*Wunderbaar.* I'll take you over to the Troyer's old place first thing tomorrow," Timothy said. "Right now, though, I bet you'll be happy to hear that Mary's making meatloaf and mashed potatoes for supper. I reckon she's invited Carolanne to stay too."

"That sounds *gut.*"

The crickets chirped loudly as Samuel and Carolanne strolled along the path near his uncle's pasture. All was quiet, except for a slight breeze rustling through the maple trees behind his uncle's barn and a dog barking somewhere off in the distance. His uncle owned a nice spread, much larger than what was currently available in Pennsylvania. That had been another reason coming to Ohio was a *gut* idea, although he would have been perfectly content to stay in Pennsylvania had circumstances been different.

Samuel glanced over at Carolanne, who had been contently walking by his side without a word. She was just as pretty as Samuel had remembered. Under her *kapp,* her blonde tresses shined in the moonlight, which also seemed to bring out her sky blue eyes. *Jah,* he knew Carolanne would help greatly in taking his mind off of Hannah.

"I'm glad you came back, Samuel. Why didn't you let me know you were coming in your last letter?" Carolanne wondered aloud.

"Uh…it was kind of a last minute decision," he explained awkwardly.

"Mary said your folks didn't know you were coming either. Not until this morning. What made you leave so suddenly?" she asked suspiciously.

Samuel blew out a breath. There was no way he was going to tell Carolanne about Hannah and ruin his chances with her. "I was anxious to start a new life out here. I enjoy my uncle's family. And I'm closer to you now." *It wasn't exactly a lie*, Samuel told himself.

Carolanne's suspicions subsided when Samuel smiled reassuringly and took her hand in his. She was so happy that Samuel had come and had been dreaming about this for nearly a year now. Since she'd first met him, she'd thought he was the most handsome man she'd ever seen. After they'd ridden in his buggy and talked for hours, she'd been able to tell Samuel was a *gut,* kind man – ideal husband material. From his conversation at the dinner table with Timothy, Carolanne gathered that the two of them were going to look at property tomorrow. Did Samuel have in mind to buy a place right away? And if so, did that mean he intended to ask her to marry him soon. Oh, Carolanne hoped it was so!

SIX

November, the following year...

Christian pulled his suspenders up over his chest, fastened his black vest, and put on his *for-gut* jacket. A sigh of relief escaped his lips. He and Hannah were finally getting married. Although they had planned on marrying the previous year, circumstances seemed to prevent the event from taking place. He knew he was blessed to be marrying Hannah at all, and that he didn't deserve her. He'd almost lost her a year ago when she found out he was also seeing an *Englisch* girl. *Jah,* he had been a *dummkopp,* he knew now.

Samuel had left over a year ago to marry his beloved Carolanne. They were all surprised when Samuel just up and left without saying goodbye to anyone. Well, he did leave a brief note. *Christian, I hope you and Hannah will be happy. I'm leaving for Ohio today and intend to ask Carolanne to marry me. Thank you for being a* gut *friend. Goodbye, Samuel.* At least he had left on amicable terms. Christian knew his friend had been disappointed in him when he'd cheated on Hannah.

He wished Samuel were here now. He missed him. Samuel had never been anything but a good, faithful, caring friend. Christian could really use some advice on how to be *gut* husband. He was certain that Carolanne had gotten a *gut* man when she married Samuel. And from the occasional letters Samuel's brother had shared with him, he knew he was doing well out in Ohio.

Hannah had troubles of her own and that was a big part of why they didn't marry last year. Christian was convinced he was the cause of it. As soon as Hannah had found out about his betrayal with the *Englisch* girl, it seemed as though her life spiraled out of control and her health took a turn for the worse. Some unknown sickness had taken a hold of her, and then it appeared as though a cloud of depression hung over her for months. It almost seemed as though the life had been drained out of her. Christian had no idea how to help her. He'd apologized many times, but somehow, he knew that wasn't enough. If he had realized what his actions would put Hannah through, he wouldn't have thought twice about the *Englisch* girl.

Now, he just wanted to be the husband that Hannah deserved.

As he joined Hannah in the upstairs hallway of her folks' home, ready to descend the stairs and begin their new life together, he could still sense Hannah's pain. She smiled, but it never fully reached her eyes and brighten her whole face as it had the day he'd asked her to marry him – a week before she'd found out. With all his heart, he wished he could erase the mistakes he had made, but that power didn't lie within his hands.

He drew Hannah close and held her for several minutes, silently communicating his love for her.

Trust, once lost, could not be easily found. Not in a year, perhaps not even in a lifetime. But Christian would do his best to regain the trust he'd lost. Somehow, someday, he would make it all up to her.

You can do this. Hannah mentally recited the mantra to herself over and over again. This was the original plan, wasn't it? It shouldn't come as a surprise. She would marry Christian. Samuel would go to Ohio and marry Carolanne. Why, then, did she feel so out of touch with reality? Why did she feel like she was stuck in a tiny room with no air left to breathe? Why did she feel like she was making the worst, *make that the second worst,* decision of her life?

She closed her eyes and took a deep breath, recalling Samuel's last words to her. She'd heard them in her head many times over the last year, "I love you, Hannah." She'd clung to those words for weeks hoping that perhaps Samuel would return, but she knew now those words had been a lie. Samuel had deserted her at a time when she needed him most. She had given him her heart and he disregarded it as though it had been a filthy rag.

How could she do this? How could she go through with it? *Gott, help me. I don't know what I'm doing. What am I supposed*

J. E. B. Spredemann

to do? She didn't know why she was praying. Surely God's ears weren't open to her prayers anymore.

As Christian took her hand, she realized it was too late to back out now. His smile brought a small amount of comfort, but she knew nothing could heal her wounded soul.

Perhaps a new start would be best. She would simply choose to forget about the past, bury it as best as she could, and hope the skeletons didn't come back to haunt her. Hannah pasted on a smile and said the words required to become Mrs. Christian Glick. Yes, she and Christian would have a good life together. She was determined to make it a reality.

42

SEVEN

Christian worried as he sat at the breakfast table alone, sipping on the coffee he'd brewed himself. It was five thirty and Hannah was still in bed. It seemed she'd been sick to her stomach every day for nearly a week now. What could be wrong with her? Christian had suggested seeing the *Englisch* doctor, but Hannah would have none of it. Well, today he was determined that she would see somebody about her illness.

Christian rose from the table and placed his coffee mug into the sink with the other dishes that now piled up, knowing Hannah would tend to them later. He walked back to their bedroom to check on Hannah one more time before going out to the barn. His eyes swept over the contoured body under the quilt his mother had made and given them as a wedding gift. Christian's gaze rested on her face. *My sweet Hannah.*

Christian couldn't have hoped for a better wife. Every day he gave thanks that she was in his life. Christian worked extra hard just so he could allow her to buy nice things. He wanted her to have anything she desired. Sometimes he wished he could go to a jewelry store and purchase something extra fancy for her, but that was not their way. He hoped she knew how much he loved her.

Hannah stirred under the blankets, but her eyes remained closed. A moan escaped her lips and Christian rushed to her side. He gently stroked her hair and placed a soft kiss on her forehead. "Sleep now, *Mei Lieb*," he whispered.

As Christian passed by the kitchen to put his boots on, he noticed the dishes again. *I'm going to wash those dishes when I come back in,* he thought. He knew Hannah wouldn't be happy about it, but she didn't need to be tending to him when she was the one that needed tending to.

After Christian finished up his chores and the dishes in the sink, he checked on Hannah again. He scribbled a note and left it on the kitchen table, should she wake up and find him gone. He was determined to bring Danika Yoder back with him so she could assess Hannah's condition. If his *fraa* refused to go to an *Englisch* doctor, he would have to bring their natural doctor to her.

Now, it was nearly five o'clock in the afternoon and Christian nervously waited for Danika to emerge from their bedroom for news of what Hannah's illness might be. Danika came into the room with an unreadable expression and Christian didn't know whether that was good or bad.

"You may go in and see Hannah now." Danika gave a slight smile.

"Is…is she all right?" Christian wrung his hands nervously.

"Just go see her. She wants to talk to you."

Oh no, this can't be good. Hannah can't be dying. Lord, please don't take Hannah from me! As Christian trudged into the room, he noticed Hannah was...*happy*?

"Hannah, what is it? *Was iss letz?*"

"Nothing is wrong, Christian," she said while taking his hand.

"Well, then...I don't understand. I thought –"

"We're going to have a baby, Christian." Illumination filled Hannah's eyes as though she'd swallowed the sunrise.

"Wha – really?" Confusion clouded Christian's face as the news registered. He couldn't have been more surprised.

Hannah nodded in affirmation.

Christian let out a sigh of relief. "*Ach*, Hannah, that's wonderful news!" Tears pricked Christian's eyes as he bent down and kissed her lips. For three years now, he'd dreamed of this moment. He and Hannah would have a little one as a testament of their love for each other. A man could have no greater honor and his heart surged with joy.

Hannah knew Christian would be excited at the news. After all, he often spoke of having his own *kinner*, especially a little boy that could work alongside him out in the field. Wasn't that every Amish man's dream? Christian was a *gut* man and he deserved to have his own *kinner*.

Although Hannah was ecstatic too, unworthiness overshadowed her excitement. She knew she didn't deserve the privilege of being a mother. She didn't deserve love. Not after all the mistakes she'd made. She was thankful nonetheless, especially for Christian's sake. This baby would surely be loved like no other.

Although pregnancies were usually kept under wraps in their community, Deborah knew Hannah was expecting. It seemed she could never, *well, almost never*, hide anything from her sister. Deborah and Peter already had a little one of their own, and to Hannah's dismay he looked just like his Uncle Samuel. Hannah had a difficult time looking at her sweet nephew. He brought back too many memories – memories she'd desperately tried to keep buried.

"As far as I can tell, you'll be having your *boppli* right around Good Friday. An Easter *boppli*, isn't that exciting?" Deb squealed.

"*Jah.* Christian is very happy," Hannah said.

"We should get started making a quilt for this little one, don't you think? *Ach*, I'm so happy Elam will have a cousin soon. I'm surprised Samuel and Carolanne haven't had any *kinner* yet."

Hannah coughed, unwilling to respond to the last comment. Truth was, she wondered if maybe God was punishing Samuel

An Unforgivable Secret

for their sin as well. But if that were true, why was *she* now expecting?

"Oh, did I tell you that Peter and I will be going out to Ohio at Christmas time to visit Samuel? We're excited to meet Carolanne. Samuel speaks so highly of her. You know she runs her own bakery. Samuel's always going on and on about her cookies. I guess she makes these delicious –"

"Deb, please." Hannah didn't know if she could stomach any more of Samuel's happy life. After keeping thoughts of him tucked away for so long, she didn't think she'd be bothered this much. Perhaps it was just her hormones. She'd heard that women in the family way could sometimes be emotional. "I…I'm not really feeling all that well."

"I thought you were through with your morning sickness."

"*Nee*, I still get it sometimes."

"You may lie down if you'd like. Samuel's old room is empty, although some of his things are still in there. I can –"

"*Ach, nee.* I'll be fine. Really. Uh, I should probably be going soon." The last thing she needed was to be in Samuel's room among his personal belongings…breathing in his scent… remembering the brief time they'd shared together and all that she'd lost. Hannah closed her eyes attempting to block the memories that now assaulted her once again. Would they ever go away?

"Going? But you just got here. Hannah, are you okay? You've been acting kind of *ferhoodled*. Is there something you'd like to tell me?" Deborah said suspiciously.

47

"*Nee*," she said emphatically.

Deborah placed a hand on her shoulder. "You know, Hannah. You can talk to me about anything. If you want to talk –"

"*Denki*, Deb. I appreciate that. But I really am fine. This *boppli* just has me so emotional about everything."

"I completely understand. I was that way with Little Sam – Elam. It seems he's got himself a new nickname, with him looking so much like his Uncle Samuel and all." Deborah laughed. "I think Samuel will be pleased to see that his nephew looks so much like him, especially since he and Carolanne don't have any *kinner* yet. It'll be a shame if they end up not being able to have any."

Hannah sighed. It seemed nearly impossible keeping feelings of Samuel at bay when her sister was constantly talking about him. *No, I need to think of Christian, my husband.* "Christian's really excited about this *boppli* coming," Hannah blurted out.

"And you, Hannah? Are you excited too? I keep hearing you say how happy Christian is, but I haven't heard you once say that you're happy." Deb raised an eyebrow.

"Uh...well, of course I'm happy. I'm just a little nervous, I guess," Hannah recovered.

"Yes, I guess it can be scary being in the family way for the first time." Deborah laughed. "Listen to me, talking as if I'm an old pro when I've only had one *boppli*. I'm sure everything will be just fine and you'll be holding that baby in your arms before you know it."

"*Jah*, you're probably right," Hannah said agreeably. As a wave of nausea hit, Hannah's hand flew to her mouth.

"Hannah, *kumm*, you really ought to lay down." Deborah took Hannah's elbow, gently pulling her toward Samuel's old room.

Hannah didn't protest this time. She realized it probably would do her some good to rest a bit. When they entered Samuel's room, relief flooded over her. The room looked like any other room in an Amish home: a simple bed topped with a quilt, a bureau with several drawers, a rack on the wall for clothing, and a simple nightstand next to the bed.

Perhaps, Hannah thought, if she could just lie down and sleep for a bit she wouldn't think of their past. After Deb closed the door to go prepare ginger tea to help with Hannah's nausea, she leaned back on the bed and closed her eyes. *I'm not going to think of Samuel*, she told herself. Several minutes later, Hannah gave up her futile attempt at sleep. It seemed nearly impossible when she just wasn't tired. She'd never been able to sleep during the day unless she was really sick.

Hannah unwittingly allowed her eyes to roam around the room. Nothing in the room pointed to Samuel: there were no clothes or hats out, no papers or Bible to identify that this was indeed his room. In fact, it could have been anybody's room. At least that's what Hannah thought until her eye caught something. She had missed it before, but now it stood out like iron pyrite shimmering under a clear stream. It stared at Hannah from inside the drawer, boring its eyes into her. Just some hay, *jah*, that's all it appeared to be. But the longer Hannah lay on the bed, the more intense the hay called to her.

This is silly, she told herself. *Why am I so drawn to some old hay?* Just to prove to herself that she was overreacting, Hannah stood from the bed and went to the bureau. She reached for the knob and pulled the drawer open. She didn't know what she was expecting, but it hadn't been this. Her breath caught as she gently lifted the small hay doll out of Samuel's drawer. *Samuel kept this?* Hannah's hands affectionately stroked the doll's plain face as sweet memories of time with Samuel bombarded her consciousness. Carefully examining the doll, Hannah noticed something on the underside that hadn't been there before. At arm's length it appeared to be a dark spot, but when Hannah examined it closer she realized Samuel had written her name on the doll. Why had Samuel kept this?

"Feeling better?" Deborah's voice called from the door.

Hannah hadn't even realized she had come in. She quickly brushed the tears from her eyes and set the doll on the dresser. "*Ach, jah.* I couldn't sleep."

"What's that ya got there?" Deborah's eyebrows lifted in curiosity.

"Aw, nothing really. Just an old hay doll I found in the drawer," Hannah answered.

"The one with your name on it?" Deb said knowingly.

Hannah's face heated. "How did you know?"

"I saw it when I was packing up Samuel's things to go in the attic. I left it there on purpose." Deborah smiled. "Sometimes

I come in here to look at it, remembering all the *gut* times we had as *kinner*. What I can't understand is why Samuel had it."

Hannah said nothing.

"Hannah, I know you and Samuel were close," Deborah divulged.

Oh no, please, God. Deborah can't know. "*Jah*, we were *gut* friends," Hannah deflected.

"I think you were more than that. Just be honest, Hannah. You and Samuel had feelings for each other that went beyond friendship. I'm guessing that's why he left for Ohio so abruptly, *jah*? Maybe he didn't want to come between you and Christian?"

Hannah shrugged.

"Hannah..." Deborah hesitated. "Are you and Christian not happy?"

"*Ach, nee.* We are happy," Hannah insisted.

"This is the life God chose for you, Hannah. You and Christian have a *boppli* on the way. You should be content; you have a *gut* life. Don't wish for something that will never be." Deborah gently touched Hannah's arm. "I want to see you smile again."

Tears filled Hannah's eyes as she embraced her younger sister. "*Denki,* Deb. I needed to hear that. I will try to be thankful for what *Gott* has given me."

EIGHT

Dat and *Mamm* ushered Hannah through the door as though she were delicate spun glass. They loved all of their *kinskinner*, but it seemed like they'd had to wait an eternity for Hannah to conceive. Each of their other daughters had gotten pregnant in the first year of marriage, so it was a bit surprising when Hannah hadn't. And even more alarming was when there was still no sign of grandchildren over the next two years. Miriam had worried that perhaps their marital relations were strained, especially during their first year of marriage when they seemed to struggle, but Hannah had protested to the contrary. Notwithstanding, they were ecstatic about another grandchild.

Mamm noticed how Christian's countenance lit up whenever the *boppli* was mentioned, but it appeared Hannah lacked the same enthusiasm. This concerned *Mamm* greatly and she hoped that Hannah wasn't slipping into depression again. There had only been one other time she had been like this and that was when she and Christian were going through a patch of rough water.

Miriam tried hard not to blame Christian, but often her efforts were futile, at least on the inside. They all knew what Christian had done and at the time they'd counseled Hannah against marrying him. However, Christian eventually proved himself worthy and regained Hannah's trust, along with the rest of the family's.

Sometimes Miriam felt that Christian went overboard in his affections for Hannah, but she was glad that her daughter had a husband who cherished her. *Mamm* was certain now that he would make a *gut* father for their grandchild.

Christian and Hannah now sat around the dinner table with *Mamm* and *Dat.* "When is your appointment with the midwife?" Miriam asked.

"She'll come by next week. I'll be about ten weeks along then," Hannah said.

"I'm so glad you'll be having a *boppli* after all this time. Just wait until you get to hold the little one in your arms. There's nothing more precious than holding a newborn baby." Miriam smiled.

"*Ach*, I can't wait." Christian's face brightened. "I wish Hannah's time was up already and I could hold our little one tomorrow." He reached for Hannah's hand across the table and gave a gentle squeeze.

"*Jah, Sohn.* I'm afraid the waiting is the hard part. But before you know it, you'll be up all night changing diapers and pacing the floor with a crying baby," Silas chimed in.

"I look forward to it." Christian smiled. "Just to be able to see a child of our own making and hold him in my arms will be the biggest blessing I could ever have, other than my beautiful *fraa*, that is."

"*Jah, kinner* are definitely a blessing from *Der Herr*," Silas said.

A blessing I'm not worthy of, Hannah thought.

Hannah glanced at the clock on the wall. The beautiful timepiece had been an engagement gift from Christian. It was intricately carved from oak wood and engraved with a scripture: As for me and my house, we will serve the Lord. *Am I serving the Lord?* Hannah wondered. Yes, she attended meeting every other week and Christian read the Bible aloud every evening in their home, but she didn't really feel like she was serving the Lord. She didn't think she'd been serving herself, though. No, she'd had too much self-condemnation for that. So who was she serving? Christian, perhaps? That wasn't necessarily a bad thing, was it? After all, wives were supposed to honor their husbands.

Perhaps she should spend more time with the other ladies in their community? Growing up, she'd gotten along just fine with everyone, but her closest friends were Christian and Samuel, and to some degree, her sister Deborah. One of the reasons she'd recently shied away is the fact that everyone else her age, it seemed, were having babies. But now that she was expecting, she felt as though she was now part of the club, so to speak. Hannah smiled as she determined to attend the next ladies' gathering.

A knock on the back door brought excitement and her stomach turned a nervous flip. Chloe was here. She'd been looking forward to this visit for a couple of weeks now, and she knew Christian was equally excited, if not even more so. She would need to call him in from the fields.

Hannah quickly opened the door for Chloe and welcomed her into the house. She noticed Christian jogging in from the fields, and caught the excitement on his face even from this distance. *He'll be a* gut *father,* Hannah had to smile at the thought.

"Christian is coming in from the fields now," Hannah informed Chloe. "Is it all right if he is here for the visit?"

"Of course. I encourage all fathers to be present during exams, but many Amish fathers feel uncomfortable. The *Englisch* fathers tend to be much less reserved about attending their wives' exams and births. I'm glad Christian wants to be with you. I can understand his enthusiasm, given you've had to wait so long for this little one."

"*Jah,* I'm afraid we won't make it another seven months, though. We're so excited," Hannah said.

"We always want things to happen sooner, but I'm afraid that part isn't up to us. Remember, God's timing is perfect." Chloe smiled, thinking of God's providence in her own life.

"*Jah*, it is," Hannah said, then remembered her manners. "Would you like some cinnamon buns and a cup of tea now, or would you like to wait until afterward."

"*Ach*, that sounds *wunderbaar*, but I never take anything until after I've first given. Shall we get started?" Chloe teased.

"Don't start without me!" Christian said, entering the kitchen.

"We weren't just yet, but now that you're here we can begin," Chloe said. "Are you ready to hear this little one's heartbeat?"

Christian's and Hannah's faces lit up. "*Ach*, we'll really be able to hear him?" Christian asked in disbelief.

Chloe nodded in affirmation, thinking how fun it was to attend new parents. Helping families grow never got old and she loved seeing others in her community blessed with new additions. She knew firsthand how much joy little ones could bring.

As Chloe placed the portable Doppler device over Hannah's still-flat abdomen, a whooshing sound echoed through the microphone. Christian held Hannah's hand as she laid on the bed and Chloe noticed tears in the corners of their eyes. Surely this babe would be born into a good family.

NINE

*C*hristian walked the row of corn and whistled happily as he thought about Hannah's appointment last week. It had been so *gut* to hear the heartbeat of their very own *boppli*. It seemed more real now that they could actually hear evidence of life. He was certain the birth of this little one would bring him and Hannah closer together. Hannah had been more her normal self lately and Christian loved seeing the sparkle in her eye again. He sent up a prayer of thanksgiving to God once again. He was more content than he'd ever been in his life and joyfulness overflowed from his soul.

Christian often wondered about Samuel and how his life was going. He wished Samuel would have brought his wife back and settled here in Pennsylvania instead of Ohio. He missed having his best friend to talk to. He and Samuel had always been so close, it almost felt as though they were brothers. It surprised Christian that Samuel never sent any letters to him and he couldn't help but feel that perhaps Samuel held some animosity toward him. Of course, Christian hadn't sent any letters to Samuel either, it just wasn't his way. He didn't really care much for letter writing.

As Christian pondered the situation, he determined that he would drop a note to Samuel in the mail. He wouldn't write much, just a simple greeting and an invitation to visit. Hopefully, Samuel would write back and eventually come visit. Christian was certain Samuel's family would love to see him as well.

A crow's call from above drew his attention to the sky. The warm sun felt *gut* on his face and he realized it was nearing time for lunch. He decided to go in a little early to see if maybe Hannah would let him help with lunch preparations, although she rarely allowed him to assist her in the kitchen. No, she was adamant the kitchen was her domain.

When Christian entered the back door, Hannah was doubled over in apparent pain. Christian quickly rushed to her side. "Hannah, what's wrong? Are you okay? Is it the *boppli*?" Fear tore through Christian's insides as he noticed Hannah's blanched face.

"I..." Hannah could barely get the words out as she clenched her abdomen tightly. "Christian, the baby!" she screamed.

Christian scooped Hannah up into his arms and rushed her to their bedroom, gently setting her on the bed. He bent down and kissed her forehead in an attempt to reassure the both of them. "Hannah, is there something I can do for you?" He looked on helplessly. "Will you be all right here by yourself for a little bit while I go fetch Chloe?"

Hannah nodded in obvious anguish.

Christian hated to leave her, but flew out the door as quickly as he possibly could and hooked up the buggy in record time. It was times like this he wished he owned a cell phone. The nearest telephone shanty was a mile away and Christian determined that he would ask the bishop if he could install one in their barn for emergencies. Christian chided himself for not thinking of that sooner.

He arrived back at the house with Chloe in tow twenty minutes later. Now, he nervously paced the living room floor waiting for Chloe's assessment. He'd chosen to stay out of the way so Chloe could work unhindered. The last thing she needed was a frantic husband bothering her when attempting to perform her duties. *Dear* Gott, *Please let Hannah and the* boppli *be okay. Please help us through whatever trials come our way, Lord. Thy will be done. Amen.*

"Christian, you may come see Hannah now," Chloe called from the bedroom door.

Christian reluctantly walked toward the bedroom, unsure of whether he wanted to hear the pronouncement that awaited him. But putting off the inevitable didn't make sense, so he walked into the bedroom with an ounce of hope that maybe his misgivings were wrong. One look at Hannah's stricken face gave Christian his answer: they had lost the baby.

Christian felt like crumbling to the floor and breaking down where he stood, but Hannah desperately needed him now. He would remain strong for Hannah's sake and grieve alone in silence. He swallowed his own grief and rushed to Hannah's side.

Chloe had discreetly exited the room, giving them time alone. Hannah sobbed in silence as he held her close to his chest, allowing her tears to fall freely. Knowing how much his own heart agonized, he couldn't imagine the heartache Hannah was now experiencing. *Please comfort Hannah, Lord. And someday, please give us a child to love. I don't know what Your will is, Lord, but I trust you. Heal our broken hearts. Amen.*

Hannah knew that it was probably her fault. Surely God was punishing her for her past sins. She was grieved, mostly for Christian's sake, but she wasn't surprised at the outcome. She had hoped, though, that God would overlook her iniquity for Christian's benefit, but it wasn't to be. Perhaps God would allow her to conceive again and He would have mercy on her the second time around.

In the weeks that passed, Hannah and Christian came to terms with the loss of their first child. They still grieved some, but Christian realized that God was in control. He continually comforted Hannah, and in doing so, he hoped they would soon be blessed with another child. It seemed the loss of the *boppli* had brought them closer together, and for that, Christian was thankful.

Chloe had explained that miscarriage was not an uncommon occurrence and in most cases, the cause of a miscarriage was often mysterious even to specialists. She'd also told them that common belief was that there was most likely something wrong with the baby and it probably wouldn't have gone to full term anyhow. Christian and Hannah were saddened to hear that sometimes women miscarried more than once, but they chose to hope for the best for future pregnancies. All in all, they knew it was all in God's hands and it was up to Him to preserve a life if He chose to.

TEN

Samuel reached over and squeezed Carolanne's hand, attempting to offer reassurance. The buggy wheel hit a rut in the dirt road, thrusting Carolanne forward, and she clenched her middle. She'd been experiencing pain on and off for a while, but lately her discomfort had become more frequent, and Samuel insisted she see the doctor. After having been married nearly four years without any children, Samuel hoped the doctor had good news for them. He was quite certain that Carolanne was expecting a *boppli*. What else could it be?

Carolanne had said she didn't think she could be in the family way, especially since her monthly cycle had never been regular. It seemed to Samuel that her symptoms pointed in that direction, though. With her lower back aching, her belly seemingly a bit larger than normal, along with her other symptoms, it just made perfect sense. Samuel had even read about it while thumbing through one of the pregnancy books his aunt Mary kept in their bookshelf.

Samuel smiled at the thought of finally becoming a father. He'd been worried that perhaps there was something wrong with him or Carolanne because they had yet to conceive. Most couples their age had at least two or three *kinner* already. But instead of taking matters into their own hands, they'd decided to trust the Lord.

It seemed Samuel had learned to do that quite a bit since coming out to Ohio. He had never been certain of his eternal destination until sitting down one night with Carolanne, Mary, and Timothy. When he realized it only took one sin to keep him out of Heaven, he knew he was in trouble. Surely he'd committed hundreds, if not thousands, of sins. Timothy had explained how simple salvation was: one only needed to believe in Christ and trust Him alone for salvation. Up until then, Samuel realized that he'd been trusting in his own works to get into Heaven. After all, he felt he was a pretty decent Amish man and hadn't made too many really bad mistakes. Well, except for with Hannah. But he realized that when he asked Jesus to save him, even *that* sin was washed away and forgotten by God. If only he could forget it too...

It had been twelve weeks since Hannah lost their first baby and Christian hoped another *boppli* would soon come to occupy the emptiness in their home and in their hearts. His hope intensified when Hannah rushed to the bathroom during breakfast, three days in a row now. He was quite certain she was in the family way again.

Today, they would pay a visit to the midwife. If Hannah was indeed in the family way, Christian wanted her to be seen as quickly as possible. The sooner she began taking her pregnancy herbs, the better chance she would have at a healthy pregnancy.

Christian leaned over and gave Hannah a kiss before descending the buggy to help her down. He knew she was just as excited about this potential pregnancy as he was, but her eyes held fear. Christian suspected that somehow Hannah felt responsible for the loss of their first child. She'd never voiced anything, but there was something about the way she reacted when he reassured her that it was God's will. He didn't know what else he could do to reassure Hannah. He hoped, for both their sakes, that a second child would heal their brokenness and give Hannah back the confidence she once possessed.

"She's definitely in the family way," Chloe proudly announced, showing them both the results of Hannah's pregnancy test.

"That's *wunderbaar*!" Christian exclaimed, grasping Hannah's hand a little tighter. Hannah only gave a slight smile.

"Are you feeling all right, Hannah?" Chloe asked, her face darkening with concern.

"*Ach, jah.* I'm fine. Just a little worried, I guess."

"Are ya thinkin' about the last one you lost?" Chloe asked, sympathy in her voice.

"*Jah*, I don't want to lose this one too," Hannah answered candidly as tears threatened.

"I really wish I could tell you that you won't, but I'm afraid I have no control over that. We have to trust *Der Herr* to know what's best," Chloe said. "Meanwhile, you do your best to stay healthy, follow the diet suggested by Danika Yoder, and take the herbs she's recommended. We've had many healthy pregnancies and *bopplin* in this district, and I'm convinced her protocol has a lot do with it."

"*Jah*, I will do that," Hannah said.

A sickening feeling turned in Samuel's gut as the doctor's grim expression met his eyes. The doctor shook his head. "I'm sorry Mr. and Mrs. Beachy; I wish I had good news for you. Carolanne is not expecting a baby."

"That is okay," Samuel reassured himself mostly. "But why has she been having these pains then?"

"I'm afraid the prognosis is not good. Carolanne has Stage Four Ovarian Cancer. It has metastasized to her liver and abdomen. Even with the best treatments we have available, the statistics aren't promising," the doctor sympathized.

"We are simple people, Doctor. We have not been to your colleges. What does all that mean?" Samuel asked unabashedly.

"It means that Carolanne is very sick and she will probably die soon. We can still treat her, but her chances of survival are slim."

No, please, Lord. It can't be. "My wife...she is going to die?" Samuel's eyes filled with tears and he embraced Carolanne, who seemed to possess a strength Samuel did not. What happened to happily ever after? What happened to growing old together and raising *kinner* and *grosskinner*?

"It is okay, Samuel. I will get to see Jesus soon," Carolanne reassured him.

"Yes, well," the doctor interjected. "I advise you to begin treatments right away."

"*Nee*, I will not have any treatments," Carolanne insisted. "You said even with treatment, I will probably still die. These treatments will make me sick, *jah*?"

"I'm afraid so, Mrs. Beachy," the doctor said.

"I don't feel too bad now. I think I can handle the pain, but I don't want the last days of my life with Samuel to be filled with sickness."

"I understand, Ma'am. Let me give you a prescription for the pain, just in case it becomes too unbearable."

"Nothing is unbearable, Doctor. God promised not to give me more than I can handle. I will trust Him for my comfort." Carolanne smiled up at Samuel.

"My *fraa* is a strong woman. *Denki*, Doctor, for your services." Samuel shook the man's hand.

"I hope all goes well with you." The doctor nodded as he exited the examining room.

After the doctor left the room, Samuel contemplated the situation in silence while Carolanne fastened her dress. *What will*

I do if Carolanne dies? He trusted the Lord, but he felt like he should *do* something. Something special. *Carolanne has been such a blessing to me. If only...*

That's when an idea popped into his head. Samuel smiled down at Carolanne.

"What are you so happy about?" she asked.

"Just thinking of my *wunderbaar fraa* and the blessing she is to me." He placed an arm around her shoulder. "What do you want, Carolanne?"

"What do you mean?" Her pretty blue eyes flashed a questioning look.

"If you could have anything, go anywhere, do anything, what would it be?" he asked.

"*Nix,* I just want to be with you, Samuel. I could be happy anywhere, doing anything, as long as I'm with you."

"But if you could? Is there nothing you've wanted to do, a dream maybe?"

"*Ach,* there's one thing. It's silly, though." She quickly dismissed her thought. "Why do you want to know?"

He ignored her question and pressed further. "Tell me, *Fraa.* Please."

Carolanne couldn't resist Samuel's sweet puppy dog eyes. "I've always wanted to see the sunset over the ocean," she said dreamily. "I told you it was silly."

"*Nee,* it's not silly. We will go." Samuel determined.

"But we'll have to go all the way to the West coast," she protested.

Samuel smiled. "We will go."

ELEVEN

Samuel opened up his wallet and paid the driver after he and Carolanne stepped out of the vehicle. With new luggage rolling behind them, they walked up to the ticket counter to purchase their plane tickets. The airport was quite different than Samuel had imagined. He expected it to be more like the train depot or bus station, but discovered it to be much larger. This was his first time ever in an airport and, he had to admit, it was a bit overwhelming.

After asking one of the airport workers for directions to their gate, they anxiously stood in line to board the plane. Samuel glanced out the large window to the tarmac where a huge passenger jet awaited. He saw the passengers at the front of their line ascending steps to board the large aircraft.

Samuel smiled down at Carolanne and grasped her hand. While their people didn't show much by way of public displays of affection, Samuel saw no harm in openly holding his *fraa's* hand. If she was as nervous as he was about boarding an aircraft for the first time, he knew she appreciated the comforting gesture. Although his trust was in *Der Herr* for their safety, he couldn't help but feel a bit apprehensive about soaring amidst the clouds. After all, if it was God's will for humans to fly, wouldn't he have given them wings?

It surprised Samuel how easy it had been to obtain permission from the bishop to fly. Normally, air travel was *verboten* and only allowed in extreme circumstances. Thankfully, their bishop was a compassionate man and he empathized with Samuel's plight. Samuel felt it was the least he could do for his sweet wife, and the thought of losing her greatly pained his heart.

Since Samuel knew the Fisher family in his former church district had relatives in California, he had asked Minister Fisher for help in locating a driver. It just so happened that Joanna and Caleb Scott, sister and brother-in-law to Minister Fisher, resided in the Bay Area. Minister Fisher's sister had married an *Englischer* years ago and they'd become missionaries in Central America. Just recently, they'd retired from the foreign mission field and began a missions ministry in Northern California.

"How was your flight?" Caleb asked glancing over his shoulder to his passengers in the back seat.

"I enjoyed it more than I thought I would, but I must admit I am happy to have my feet back on solid ground," Samuel replied.

"Well, I don't know how solid the ground is. You know this place is known for its earthquakes," Caleb teased.

"Don't let him scare you," his wife Joanna chimed in. "We do get earthquakes, but they aren't all that common."

"Samuel tells me you have relatives in Pennsylvania," Carolanne added.

"*Jah*, my folks and brothers and sister live in Paradise. My younger brother Jonathan is a minister now." Joanna laughed. "I never imagined my mischievous little brother becoming a preacher. He was always into some kind of trouble when we were growing up!"

"Sounds like my brother and I," Samuel commented.

"So you used to be Amish too, then?" Carolanne asked continuing her conversation with Joanna.

"Yes. I never planned on leaving, but it turned out that God had other plans for me," Joanna said.

Caleb gave Joanna's hand a gentle squeeze. "And boy, am I glad for that! I couldn't have been blessed with a better help-meet. God knew how much I needed her."

"I am the one that's blessed," Joanna insisted. "And thank you for asking us to drive you. We haven't been to San Simeon and Cambria in years. We kind of spent our second honeymoon there. It will be nice to go back."

"This beautiful drive is amazing, but I can't wait to get there." Carolanne glanced out the window of the sedan, watching the Pacific Ocean as they traveled. She tried not to let the speed at which they traveled bother her. Riding gently along in a buggy was one thing she loved about the Plain lifestyle. "I've always dreamed of sitting on the beach and watching the sun set over the ocean."

"Well, believe me, you won't be disappointed. It's beautiful," Joanna said. "And romantic."

Carolanne smiled at Samuel, thinking how blessed she was to have such a sweet, caring husband. "Will we be there in time to see it tonight?"

"We should be able to catch it after checking in to the motel," Caleb said. "And after that, maybe we can enjoy a nice dinner at the Cavalier. I love their sourdough bread bowls filled with clam chowder." He licked his lips.

"That sounds good to me," Samuel said. "I could use a *gut* meal."

"We'll go to the Main Street Grill in Cambria tomorrow," Caleb said wiggling his eyebrows at Samuel in the rear view mirror.

Joanna laughed. "Is eating all you ever think about?"

"I'm a growing boy, what can I say?" Caleb raised his hands in protest, then quickly placed them back on the steering wheel so as not to frighten his passengers. Being considerate of others in the car was one thing that Joanna had taught him. He'd never considered how frightening traveling in a car at high speeds could be until he met his wife, who'd rarely been in cars before meeting him.

Samuel and Carolanne chuckled, enjoying the playful banter between Joanna and Caleb.

"Do you have any plans for sightseeing while you're here?" Caleb asked Samuel.

"*Ach*, I really didn't think much about it, other than spending time with my *fraa*," Samuel said. "Do you have any suggestions?"

"Well, let's see. There's Hearst Castle. We've never been there before, but have heard it's pretty amazing," Caleb said.

"Really? A castle?" Samuel's interest piqued.

"Yes, there was a wealthy man, William Randolph Hearst, who owned several publications. He hired an architect and I've heard he even had some stone pillars imported from Rome or Greece or somewhere. Anyway, it's supposed to be something to see. There's a free visitors' center, if you'd like to go check it out one of these days."

Samuel looked to Carolanne for approval. "*Jah*, we'd like to see that if it's not too much trouble."

"The elephant seals are a pretty interesting sight, as well. And you two will love the Fiscalini Trail," Caleb said. "There's an old school house over by Sebastian's Store in San Simeon that reminds me of an Amish school. You should check that out too."

"Caleb, I'm sure they'll want to relax some while they're here too." Joanna laughed.

"I don't want Carolanne to overdo it. This trip is for her, so whatever she wants to do is fine with me," Samuel said. He leaned over to Carolanne, and gently grazed her cheek with his lips, out of sight of the front passengers.

"I'd like to do all of that if I'm up to it," Carolanne said with a smile, intertwining her fingers with her husband's.

Several hours later, as the sun faded into the horizon, Carolanne sat contentedly on the beach. With Samuel's strong arms wrapped around her, she soaked in the last few rays of sunshine to the sound of crashing waves. The sun's warmth turned into a chilly breeze as the sky rapidly darkened.

"Joanna was right. This is romantic...and beautiful," Carolanne commented.

"Nothing can compare to *Der Herr's* beauty. And I thank Him for giving me a beautiful *fraa* to enjoy His *wunderbaar* masterpiece with," Samuel said.

Carolanne smiled up at her gracious husband. "*Ich liebe dich*, Samuel."

"I love you too, Carolanne," Samuel replied. He pulled her close for a slow sweet kiss as a canopy of stars now twinkled above them.

TWELVE

Samuel had been contemplating what to do for some time now and he felt like he'd finally received his answer. Ever since Carolanne passed on several months ago, he'd been lonely. Lonely for his family back home in Pennsylvania, and he sorely missed Christian's companionship.

Although Christian had sent him a couple of letters over the past few years, he'd never felt the timing was right for a visit. Especially after he'd found out about Carolanne's illness and her impending death. He'd wanted to spend every possible moment with his *fraa* while she was alive and had even worked as little as possible to make it happen. But now that she was gone, nothing was keeping him bound to Ohio.

Samuel had thought about Hannah, and figured that enough time had gone by since he'd left. Surely Hannah was happy and secure in her marriage by now and seeing him shouldn't be a problem.

As Samuel held his brother's letter in his hand, he reread the part about Christian and Hannah. They had recently lost a second child to miscarriage and the grief had begun to take a toll on them. Samuel wasn't an expert, but he felt he could offer Christian comfort in his time of need. Losing Carolanne had been difficult, but he could see now how he'd grown through the experience. Perhaps he could bear some of Christian's burden and encourage him to trust the Lord's will.

Yes, that is what he would do. He wouldn't send a letter to announce his coming, he would just show up out of the blue and surprise everyone.

"All right, Hannah. You've been cooped up in this house way too long. It's time you got out and had a little fun," Deborah said.

"Deb, you know I don't feel like going anywhere."

Deborah sighed. "Hannah, I know you're upset about losing the *boppli*. I'm really sorry. But I hate to see my sister so sad all the time. Please just come to town with me, will you? I talked to Chloe and she said there's no reason you can't go out. Peter is watching our *kinner* and Christian doesn't have any objections, so now it's up to you. What do you say?"

"Well, I guess it would be nice to go for a drive," Hannah said agreeably.

"So, does that mean you'll go?" Deb asked with hopefulness.

Hannah shrugged unenthusiastically. "I guess it wouldn't hurt."

"Okay, Hannah. I want you to close your eyes until we get there," Deborah said.

Hannah sighed. "Deb, you know I don't like surprises."

"You'll like this one. Now stop being a *boppli* and close your eyes."

Hannah huffed then rolled her eyes. "Okay, I'll close my eyes just to make *mei schweschder* happy."

Deborah maneuvered the buggy down several unnecessary roads to throw Hannah off track so she wouldn't guess where she was taking her. When they finally arrived at their destination, Deborah instructed Hannah to open her eyes.

Hannah squinted in the sun, adjusting her eyes to the light after having them closed for too long. When she finally realized where they were, she gasped. "Deborah, we can't afford to go here," Hannah said looking up at the large Sight and Sound Theatre building.

"You don't have to afford it, Hannah. It's my treat. I've always wanted to see a play here. And I know you have too."

"But Deb –"

"There are no buts. Now get out of the buggy or you're walking home," Deborah insisted.

Hannah frowned disapprovingly at her younger sister.

"Hannah, don't you remember when we were younger and we used to pretend we were Bible characters?"

"*Jah*, I think I still have the bump on my head from the rock you threw at me when you recruited me to play Stephen."

Deborah laughed. "I can't believe you still haven't forgiven me for that. And in all fairness, you volunteered for Stephen."

"That was before you informed me that I was going to be stoned," Hannah said.

"I guess it pays sometimes to know the Bible." Deborah shrugged. She looked up and noticed people entering the theater. "Come on, Hannah. We'd better go in before we're late."

Hannah nodded and gave a slight smile. "Okay, I'll go. And by the way, I have forgiven you for the rock."

Deborah smiled and sent up a silent prayer for her sister. She really hoped this day would be a blessing to her and allow her to take her mind off her troubles.

"*Ach*, Hannah. I'm really glad you came with me today. I hope you liked it," Deborah said pulling her buggy into Hannah and Christian's country lane.

"*Jah*, I had a *gut* time. *Denki,* Deb. I really do appreciate you taking me," Hannah said.

Deborah looked ahead and noticed a buggy near the barn. "Looks like you and Christian have company."

"I wonder who it could be. It doesn't look like *Mamm's* carriage," Hannah said. "Will you stay and have some tea?"

"Maybe another time. I've got to get home and relieve Peter of the *kinner*. I'm sure little Becky's hungry by now."

"All right. I'll see ya at meeting on Sunday." Hannah waved as Deborah turned the buggy around in the yard and headed for home.

With a smile, she stepped in to the kitchen through the back door. Now that she was home, she could tell Christian all about the *gut* time she and Deborah had at the Sight and Sound Theatre. She was thankful Deborah had talked her into going. It did indeed take her mind off her troubles.

Christian walked in to the kitchen and kissed Hannah. "*Kumm*, you have to see who's here." Christian happily pulled Hannah along to the living room where their guest stood up from the rocker and turned around to face them.

Hannah didn't recognize him at first because she'd never seen him with a beard, but as soon as she looked into his eyes his identity was undeniable. Hannah swallowed hard and her smile quickly faded into a frown. "Samuel."

THIRTEEN

Samuel hadn't known what to expect from Hannah, but by her expression he gathered she was *not* thrilled to see him. Could he blame her, though? The last time he'd seen her she'd been nestled in his arms, and he'd been kissing her soft full lips. Samuel shook his head in an attempt to dispel the improper thought. He would not allow himself to think about his best friend's *fraa* in that way, regardless of what they'd shared in the past. Samuel had no intentions of ruining an already fragile marriage.

"What is *he* doing here?" Hannah asked coldly.

Christian shot her a puzzled look. "Samuel's moving back. He's going to be helping me with the harvest, so he'll be living in the *dawdi haus*."

Hannah shook her head. "Why can't he move in with Peter and Deborah?"

"I invited him to stay here. Hannah, what's wrong with you?" Christian scolded, disappointed in her somewhat insolent behavior.

Hannah spun around and stomped off toward their bedroom, to Christian's dismay. The door shut loudly behind her.

"I'm sorry, Samuel. I don't know what's gotten in to Hannah. She's usually not disrespectful. She must not be feeling well." Christian attempted to explain away his wife's odd behavior.

"Look, Christian. If it's going to be a problem, I can leave. I don't have to stay here," Samuel said regretfully.

"*Nee*, you will stay. I want you to stay, Samuel. Hannah will be fine. She's been emotional since the *boppli*..." Christian's voice trailed off.

"I understand. I just don't want to cause any trouble."

"You are my best friend. You could never be trouble," Christian said confidently. "Now about that cup of coffee we were talking about earlier."

"I'm all for it, but maybe you should go see if Hannah is all right," Samuel suggested.

"*Jah*, I will do that."

Christian gingerly opened the door to the bedroom where Hannah lay on the bed. Her back was turned toward him and he couldn't see her face. "Hannah, *Lieb*, sit up. I want to talk to you."

Hannah swiped her eyes and slowly came to a sitting position. She said nothing and stared at the floor.

"What was that all about? Why were you disrespectful to Samuel?" Christian tried to temper his voice.

Hannah squeezed her eyes closed. "How can you just let him come back like that?"

"What?"

"He left you without even saying goodbye. The whole time he was gone, he never sent you any letters. What kind of friend is that?" Hannah said. "And now, you invite him to stay with us?"

"Hannah, Samuel is our friend. He's welcome in our home any time. Whatever grudge you're holding against him, you need to let it go."

"He *was* our friend, Christian. Have you forgotten how he just up and left? Friends don't do that."

"I don't understand why that's a big deal. Yes, we missed Samuel. But we always knew he'd be going back to Ohio to marry Carolanne. That was no surprise." Christian sighed. "Hannah, it's Samuel's life. If he wanted to leave the way he did, it was his choice."

"It wasn't right," Hannah maintained.

"Hannah, it's not our place to judge. And as long as Samuel is staying in our home, I expect you to be respectful to him. He is our guest and a friend."

Hannah nodded meekly.

"If you would, I'd like you to make some coffee," Christian requested. "Samuel and I will be moving his things into the *dawdi haus.*"

Samuel looked up at Christian as he closed the door behind him and came back into the living room. He couldn't help but overhear the conversation between Hannah and Christian. To his relief, Hannah hadn't mentioned their past relationship. If she had, he was quite certain Christian's demeanor would be different.

"Let's get your things now. Hannah will be preparing us some coffee and a snack," Christian informed Samuel.

Samuel nodded. He would need to talk to Hannah alone later. Clearly, their past relationship needed closure.

Hannah took the carafe of coffee, poured the hot liquid into two mugs, and set them on the table with fresh cream and pure maple syrup. That had always been a favorite of Christian's and Hannah had to admit she enjoyed the combination as well. She had baked an oatmeal cake – Christian's favorite – early this morning and decided it would go perfectly with the coffee.

Hannah released the breath she'd been holding. Being rebuked by Christian hadn't been easy, and up until today, he'd never reprimanded her for anything. Of course, she'd never needed to be reproved for anything before. She realized now that she had indeed been rude and she regretted disappointing her husband. But she couldn't help it. How was she supposed to know that Samuel would show up out of the blue after all these years and turn her emotions inside out? In her choler, she'd been tempted to tell Christian about their past, but fortunately thought better of it before she blabbed anything she'd regret.

She decided the best thing for her to do was to avoid Samuel as much as possible. If she didn't have to look at him or talk to him, everything would be fine. She would simply pretend he wasn't there. After all, she'd become very good at pretending. And when she had to speak out of common courtesy, she would say only what was necessary.

Christian softly stroked Hannah's long hair as she lay next to him on their bed. "Hannah, I'm sorry for getting upset with you earlier today," he whispered. "*Denki* for being kind to Samuel this evening."

Hannah turned over and snuggled close to her husband. "*Denki* for saying that, Christian. I love you."

"I love you, too, *Schatzi*." Christian bent down and planted a kiss on Hannah's lips then pulled their wedding quilt up over their heads.

After breakfast, Samuel sat on a small bench just inside the back door, tying the laces on his work boots. He purposely lingered in hopes of speaking with Hannah. Since she'd been smiling this morning, he hoped it would be a *gut* time to catch her alone. He glanced out the window of the back door and noticed Christian stepping into the barn to begin morning chores. Samuel took one last swig of his coffee and neared the kitchen sink to place his empty mug on the counter. Hannah had already begun washing the breakfast dishes.

"Hannah, I wanted to say –"

"Don't you think Christian's waiting for you outside?" she spat out, clenching her hands tightly in the dish water.

"I was hoping we could talk," he said gently. Samuel wished she would just look at him and see the sincerity in his eyes. He genuinely desired to rectify past wrongs.

"I'm not interested in talking with you, Samuel. Now I think it's best that you get to work. Christian will wonder where you are," she answered curtly, then resumed her dish washing with vigor. "We wouldn't want him to think there was ever anything between us, would we?"

Samuel sighed with a heavy heart and resignedly walked to the door. Yep, he'd read her correctly. She hadn't forgiven him for leaving the way he did. He couldn't say he blamed her, though. Regaining her friendship certainly wasn't going to be easy. At least he still had Christian's friendship; fortunately, all hadn't been lost.

FOURTEEN

When Samuel entered the barn, he spied Christian near the horses' stalls. His head was bowed down and Samuel was unsure whether he was praying or not. As Samuel quietly approached, Christian lifted his head.

"I'm sorry if I interrupted," Samuel said.

"*Ach, nee*. Sometimes I just need a little quiet time. It's hard with everything Hannah and I have gone through. I'm worried about what will happen if she becomes pregnant again. She's had such a difficult time dealing with losing the other *bopplin*."

Samuel clasped Christian's shoulder. "And how about you, Christian? How are you doing?"

"I'm dealing with it the best way I know how. I'm working." He gave a half-smile. "It seems to keep my mind occupied, but it's not always easy."

"*Nee*, I'm afraid life is rarely that. Do you know what Carolanne said when the doctor offered pain medication for her cancer?" He didn't wait for a response, but continued on. "She said that *Gott* promised never to give us more than we can handle, and that she would trust Him for her comfort."

"It sounds like your Carolanne was a wise woman, and a strong one," Christian said.

"I believe her strength came from *Der Herr*. It is *that* strength that helped me through her death."

"*Jah*, I am trusting *Gott*. I worry about Hannah, though. She is not strong."

"Christian, have you and Hannah ever trusted Christ for salvation?" Samuel asked.

"I cannot speak for Hannah, but I myself have," Christian said.

"Perhaps that is why she struggles so."

"Perhaps." Christian pondered a moment, then smiled at Samuel. "*Denki*, Samuel, for coming home. I have missed your friendship."

Samuel grabbed a pitchfork and began mucking out a stall. "And I have missed yours too, Friend. Now I think we'd better get to work before Hannah refuses to feed us."

"If you don't work, you don't eat!" They both recited in unison. Christian laughed. "I don't know how many times I heard that growing up. Probably too many to count."

After Christian fetched a rake and began contently working side by side with Samuel, all became quiet, but for the sound of their working and breathing.

Hannah glanced out the window when she heard a buggy rumble up the drive. She smiled when she realized Deborah and Peter had come to visit. No doubt they'd gotten wind of Samuel's return. Hannah dried her hands and walked outside to meet her sister.

Christian and Samuel emerged from the barn as well. Hannah watched as Samuel and Peter embraced. Young Elam jumped into his uncle's arms and Samuel spun him around like an airplane. The resemblance between the two of them was remarkable and Hannah wondered, had things turned out differently, what a child of Samuel's would've looked like. At that moment, Samuel's and Hannah's eyes met and a knowing look passed between them.

Deborah grasped Hannah's hand and pulled her toward the house after offering her two brothers-in-law a quick greeting. She took her infant daughter from Peter's arms and gave her to Hannah to hold. "Hannah, Becky, and I will go round up some snacks for everyone," she informed the men.

"How did you know Samuel was here?" Hannah wondered aloud as they entered the kitchen.

"The mysterious buggy in your driveway yesterday and someone in town mentioned they thought they'd seen Samuel, so I put two and two together. I'm just wondering why he's *here*."

Hannah didn't miss Deborah's pointed look. She threw up her free hand. "Don't look at me. I was just as surprised as you are."

"So he's going to be *staying* here?" Deborah raised her eyebrows.

"Apparently." Hannah shrugged.

"And you're okay with that?"

"Deb, I don't have much of a choice. Christian invited him to stay here. I already tried protesting and it didn't work," Hannah said.

"If I were you, I'd tell Christian about your and Samuel's past relationship."

Hannah looked at her sister in horror. "*Ach, nee.* I could never tell him."

"I hope you know what you're doing, Hannah." Deborah shook her head. "Having him here in the same house isn't wise."

"He's not here, he's in the *dawdi haus.* Besides, it's not my decision to make, Deb. I try to avoid him the best I can. Other than that, there's not much I can do." The baby began fussing in Hannah's arms and she handed little Becky to her mother. "Besides, he's here for Christian, not for me."

"I really hope you're right."

Several hours after her sister had left and she'd finished cleaning up the kitchen following supper, Hannah made a beeline for the stairs, determined to stay occupied. Hannah's broom now moved slower and slower as Christian's and Samuel's cheerful voices wafted up the stairs to where she was working. She had no desire to be in Samuel's company, but couldn't help but envy the two men's camaraderie as they sat downstairs playing checkers. It used to be the three of them, but now here she was upstairs by herself while Christian and Samuel laughed downstairs. Why couldn't things just go back to the way they were before love had to come along and complicate everything?

FIFTEEN

Samuel living in the *dawdi haus* hadn't been as difficult as Hannah thought it would be. Of course, the fact that she hardly looked at him or spoke with him may have had something to do with it. She knew she still harbored bitterness toward him, but she didn't expect that to ever go away. It was simply a fact of life.

What Hannah didn't care for was the fact that Samuel was stealing away her time with Christian. Sure, they still went to bed together every night, but everything was different now. It used to be just the two of them at breakfast time talking about their day and what they had planned. Now Samuel and Christian talked about whatever the two of them were doing while Hannah sat listening politely.

Hannah placed her hand on top of her belly. She hadn't even told Christian that she was in the family way again. Maybe she would just not tell him at all. After all, God would probably take this one from her too. Perhaps it was better if Christian didn't know; it would spare him grief.

She glanced into the refrigerator trying to determine what she would prepare for dinner tonight. Christian and Samuel were already out working in the fields although the sun had barely risen. Finding nothing that appealed to her, Hannah surveyed the contents of their basement pantry. She smiled with pride at all of the canned goods she'd managed to put up during the summertime. If her estimation was correct, her lined shelves contained about four hundred jars of various fruits and vegetables. Since it was just her and Christian, she hadn't needed to put up as much as other women with large families did.

Hannah reached up to grab a couple of jars of Chow-Chow from the top shelf, when an excruciating pain suddenly ripped through her middle. She looked down to see a stream of blood pooling on the floor beneath her and immediately collapsed to the floor.

Christian lifted his hat and wiped the sweat from his brow. He laughed as his stomach rumbled loud enough for Samuel to hear. He pulled the mules to a stop and glanced back at Samuel.

"Guess it's time for lunch, *jah*?" Samuel smiled and gulped down the last of his water.

"*Jah*, let's unhitch the team," Christian agreed, stepping down from the platform on the trailer.

"What do you supposed Hannah's got for us today?" Samuel raised his eyebrows thinking of the delicious *yumaseti* they'd had yesterday.

"*Ach*, I don't know, but I'm sure it will be *gut*," Christian said, tasting the food already.

Samuel glanced toward the house then looked back at Christian with a sparkle in his eye. "Race you to the house," he challenged.

"You're on," Christian said with a boyish grin.

"One, two, th –" Before Samuel had finished the word, Christian bolted. "Hey, that's cheating!"

"Hurry up, Old Man, before I beat you," Christian hollered over his shoulder.

As Samuel and Christian clattered into the house panting, the kitchen appeared to be empty. They both moved toward the sink for a drink of water. Christian glanced at the clock, surprised that Hannah didn't have lunch out on the table yet. He walked to the stove and peered into an empty pot. Puzzled, Christian went to check if Hannah was in the bedroom but quickly realized she wasn't there either.

"Hannah," he called out but heard no response. He took the stairs two at a time to check if maybe she'd been working in one of the upstairs rooms and hadn't heard him.

"I can't find her anywhere," he said to Samuel as he descended the staircase.

"Could she be outside?" Samuel suggested.

"Why don't you go check? She may be in the garden. I'll see if she's in the basement," Christian said. "Hannah!" he called out prior to descending the steps.

When Christian hit the final step, he spotted Hannah lying on the floor in a pool of blood. He rushed over to her, but she appeared pale and unconscious. Christian hollered up the steps, "Samuel! Samuel!"

In less than a minute, Samuel flew down the stairs where he'd heard Christian calling from outside. "What's wrong?" he said before spotting Hannah on the floor. Christian gave him a helpless look and Samuel noticed the blood surrounding Hannah. "Oh no! I'll call an ambulance."

As quickly as he could, Samuel ran to the barn where Christian had installed a phone a year earlier. Within minutes, the shrill of a siren pierced the quiet countryside. Samuel sent up a silent prayer for Hannah's wellbeing.

Beep...beep...beep...beep. Hannah's eyes fluttered open and she surveyed her surroundings. She spotted the heart monitor where the noise resounded from. Christian sat on a plastic chair next to her bed and took her hand, releasing an anxious sigh.

"Hannah," he said rising from the chair and planting a kiss on her forehead. "You're awake."

"What happened?" Hannah asked, not remembering she'd collapsed in the cellar. "I...I was fixing lunch."

"Don't worry about lunch, *Lieb*," Christian reassured her. "The doctor will come in later to let us know what happened with you."

"The *boppli*, did I lose it?" Hannah frowned.

His pained expression told her all she needed to know. *Why, Lord?*

"You...you knew you were in the family way? How come you didn't tell me?" Christian asked.

"You and Samuel were so busy. I...I just didn't think you cared to know. I knew I would probably lose it anyway," Hannah said brushing away a tear.

Christian's heart broke at her words. "Oh Hannah, how could you think I wouldn't want to know about a *boppli*? I'm sorry I haven't spent much time with you lately. That will change," he promised, gently stroking her hand.

Hannah's eyes turned toward the opening door as she watched the doctor stride toward her bed. The doctor peered down at her chart. "Your husband says this is your third miscarriage. Is that correct?" His bushy brown eyebrows raised.

"*Jah*," she answered quietly.

"Why does she keep losing the babies?" Christian asked in hopes of finding a solution to her failed pregnancies.

"It's difficult to tell, but I'm guessing it has something to do with a past abortion. Her cervix –"

Hannah's head shot up.

"Her...her what?" Christian asked in confusion.

Hannah stared down at her hands. *No, God! Please. Please don't let Christian find out. He can't find out!*

The doctor continued, "Her damaged cervix indicates that a prior abortion –"

"I'm sorry, Doctor, but that can't be right. My Hannah has never had an abortion. We are Amish, we don't believe in such things," Christian stated adamantly. "Tell him, Hannah. Tell the doctor he's wrong," he said confidently.

The doctor's knowing gaze penetrated Hannah's reticent one.

Hannah swallowed hard and her guilt-ridden eyes met Christian's. She remained silent. Oh, the pain. Hannah couldn't speak.

"Hannah?" Christian looked at her in confusion, his eyes registering her shamefacedness. "It's...it's true?" His prior confidence quickly dwindled.

Hannah bowed her head and a tear trickled down her cheek.

The doctor quietly slipped out of the room to allow them privacy.

"No!" Christian dropped her hand as though it were a burning coal. He paced back and forth on the floor near her bed. "When, Hannah? When did you have an abortion?" His voice wavered.

"Before we were married," she admitted quietly.

"But we never..." Christian lifted his hat and raked a hand through his hair. His face darkened and his hands began shaking. "You...you fornicated with another man? Who?"

Hannah shook her head, refusing to divulge any more of her secret.

"Who?" he yelled, not caring if the entire hospital heard. His face burned with anger.

Hannah remained silent.

"I...I don't know what to say, Hannah." Christian's heart beat rapidly. *How could I have lived with Hannah this long and not known this? What kind of a woman did I marry? Certainly not the pure white lily I had thought – that she portrayed herself to be.*

Christian released an elongated breath. He made his decision. "I'll be moving into the *dawdi haus* with Samuel. If any of our family asks why, *you* are explaining it to them. I will no longer dwell in the same house with you. We will be married in name only. To me, you are shunned." With that, Christian turned on his heel and left the hospital.

Hannah sobbed into her palms and cried as she never had before. She'd known this is what would happen if her secret was ever divulged. It was only a matter of time before she was rejected by their entire community.

Hannah remembered the events of the past as though they had happened just yesterday. If only she could go back and do things differently...

SIXTEEN

Five years prior...

Samuel had seen Christian and Hannah go outside the barn, but he didn't think anything of it. Now, though, the singing had begun. They should've been back in by now. *He was about to get up and go search for them, when he noticed Hannah entering the barn alone. He watched as she whispered into her sister's ear. Deborah nodded and squeezed her hand. With her countenance distraught, Hannah walked out of the barn. Samuel knew he had to find out what was going on.*

A quarter mile up the road, he spotted her walking toward home. Samuel jogged to catch up with her and soon he strode by her side. "Hannah, is everything okay?"

She sobbed and brushed away a tear. "Nee, Samuel."

"If you'd like to talk, I'm here to listen," Samuel offered. "Does it have something to do with Christian? Did you two have an argument?"

Hannah quietly nodded her head. "Samuel, Christian...he's been seeing an Englisch *girl," she cried.*

Oh no. How did she find out?

"I saw them together at the restaurant last night," she explained, answering his unspoken question.

Samuel felt like he could wring Christian's neck right about now. He always feared she'd get hurt by Christian's thoughtlessness, but only now did he realize the tremendous pain it caused her. He needed to find a way to lift her spirits and cheer her up. "What are you going to do?" he wondered aloud.

"I don't know. He said he still wants to marry me, but I can't trust him anymore."

Samuel thought for a moment, pondering what might bring a smile to her beautiful face. He needed to get her mind off of Christian. "Hey, our mouse catcher had kittens a few weeks ago. Would you like to see them?"

A small smile cracked at the corner of her mouth and Samuel knew he'd found a solution, albeit temporary. "Jah, denki, Samuel."

Samuel entered the dark barn first and quickly found the lantern that hung by the door. Night had fallen outside, resulting in pitch blackness inside the barn's interior. He swiped a match and a flame emanated from the wick inside the glass dome. He'd done this so many times; he could probably do it with his eyes closed.

"The litter is up in the haymow," he explained as he stepped onto the first rung of the wooden ladder and slowly began climbing.

Hannah nodded her consent and followed him up. The haymow had always been one of her favorite places to play as a child. She and her siblings would often play hide and seek behind the large stacks of hay. She wondered if Samuel had had similar experiences.

"Did ya ever play hide and seek up here?" Hannah asked as she glanced around the spacious upper level of the barn. Lack of sufficient light prevented her from seeing more than just a few feet around them.

"Ach, jah. 'Twas a lot of fun." Samuel smiled, and then pulled a small flashlight from his pocket. "Wait here. I will bring the mouse catchers." He left the lantern near Hannah.

Hannah sat down on a bale of hay and breathed in deeply. She'd always loved the smell of sweet alfalfa. She pulled a piece of straw from the bale she sat on and placed it between her teeth, contently chewing it.

Samuel reappeared with two small kittens. One was pure white and the other was striped gray, a tabby. He held them out to her and she took the white one from his hand. She placed it into her lap and began to pet its soft fur. The kitten gently licked her fingers with its rough sandpaper-like tongue.

"Ach, this one is so cute!" she gushed.

Samuel pulled out a hay straw as well and began chewing on it. "My bruder *and I used to light the end of these and pre-*

tend we were smoking. I don't know why we did it. We would cough so bad, it was terrible." He laughed, recalling the memory. "Until one day Peter accidentally dropped his and almost caught the barn on fire."

Hannah attempted to cover a laugh with her hand. "Ach, no. Really?"

"Jah. Dat found out and gave us a whipping for it." He grimaced, still remembering the pain on his back side. "Don't tell your sister, though. Peter won't like me telling his business."

"I won't." Hannah smiled, recalling a memory of her own. "My schweschdern and I used to make hay dolls." She quickly pulled out a small handful of long straw from the bale. Samuel watched with interest as her skillful fingers bent the straw, twisting and turning it in her hands, then fastening it into what, indeed, looked like a doll. "See?" She smiled, holding up her creation.

"Jah, pretty creative. I always wondered what the maedel were doing when they were supposed to be working," he teased.

Hannah feigned offense. She playfully threw the hay doll at him and covered a giggle.

Ach, Samuel loved seeing the joy on her face once again. If only he could remove her pain forever. Samuel stroked the kitten in his lap. "Did ya know that cats can fall from really high places and not get hurt?" he asked.

"Jah, I think I read about that somewhere. Probably back when we were in school."

"Well, Peter and I tested the theory and found it to be true. We used to drop them from the haymow." Samuel chuckled. "Until one time we didn't realize that Dat *was walking below and one landed on him. Peter and I didn't fare too well that time either. It just so happened that* Dat *looked up right after we'd launched the kitten and it scratched his face up real* gut. *He sure wasn't very happy about that."*

Hannah laughed. "I can imagine. It sounds like you and Peter were an apronful of mischief."

*"Jah, we were for sure. Much more than the others," Samuel said, his eyes sparkling. "*Mamm *says we still are sometimes."*

Hannah reached over and squeezed Samuel's hand. "Den-ki, Samuel. I really needed a friend tonight."

Samuel sobered. "You know, Hannah, Christian is a gut *man." He released her hand.*

Hannah rose from the bale. "Please, Samuel, don't. I don't want to talk about Christian. He..." Her voice broke into a sob. She swallowed to stop herself from breaking down again.

Samuel went to her and gently touched her arm. "Ach, I'm sorry, Hannah." Samuel silently chided himself. He should've known better than to mention Christian's name.

Samuel is such a thoughtful, caring man. *"I wish I'd fallen in love with you instead. You're so kind, Samuel." She held his gaze, his hazel eyes glistened in the lantern light.*

Samuel stepped forward and gently stroked her cheek. "I...I care for you, Hannah." He swallowed hard. "I always have."

"Jah, *we've always been* gut *friends,*" *she said, denying her growing attraction to Samuel.*

"Nee. *What I mean is...*" *his voice trailed off as he leaned forward and pressed his lips to hers. Samuel expected resistance, but instead Hannah deepened the kiss and stepped into his embrace. Several intense moments passed.*

All Hannah wanted to do was forget about Christian and all the pain he'd caused. Samuel, she admitted to herself, was everything she'd been searching for. How is it that she'd never known...till now?

"Ach, *Hannah, you're...so...beautiful,*" *he commented while softly stroking her unbound hair that now tumbled down her back.*

Samuel reached over and dimmed the light. "Ich liebe dich, *Hannah.*"

"*I love you, too, Samuel,*" *Hannah breathed out, realizing it for the first time.*

All the pain, heartache, and disappointment Hannah had felt earlier was forgotten in Samuel's strong, loving arms. This would be a night she'd never forget. Fully knowing what their actions were leading to, neither one protested. But little did either of them realize that this one event, a single secret transgression, would permanently alter the course of many lives forever.

Several hours later, Hannah awakened. She wasn't sure, but she thought she'd felt a gentle nudge on her arm. Her eyes scanned the dimly lit barn where the lantern's glow permeat-

ed. Other than the quilt that covered her body, the only other things nearby were her clothes and prayer kapp. She hastily dressed and searched the haymow for Samuel, but apparently he'd gone.

Hannah decided to leave as well. It would not do to be found alone up in Samuel's vatter's *haymow*. If anyone ever found out...So many questions filled Hannah's mind and she wondered what the two of them would do now. And how would they tell Christian that they were in love? Certainly, this changed everything.

SEVENTEEN

Hannah had cried herself to sleep last night. Samuel was gone. When Christian told her of Samuel's note, she'd felt a mixture of sadness, betrayal, and relief all at the same time. Relieved for Christian's sake, but grieved at the finality of her and Samuel's relationship. She'd wanted to break down in tears then and there, but Christian surely would have suspected something. No, as bleak as it seemed, Christian was the only steady thing in her life right now, despite his past indiscretions, which now seemed miniscule in comparison to her own. She would cling to that lifeline now because it was all she had.

Samuel had been there when she needed him the night before last, but where was he now? Did he just expect her to go on as though nothing had happened between them, as though they hadn't shared the most intimate part of their lives with each other? How could he go now and ask Carolanne to marry him after what they'd shared? How could she marry Christian? Surely the guilt would never allow her to do such a thing.

Hannah did her best to forget Samuel and what they'd shared together, but it was impossible. She knew deep down that nothing could erase the memories. She would never forget. But she tried. Each day she would go about her normal routine, and when Samuel's image popped up she suppressed it and forced herself to think about something else.

Six weeks passed. Hannah thought she had finally succeeded in laying Samuel's memory to rest – she hadn't thought of him in days. And then it began. Hannah sat at the breakfast table with the rest of her family, but she couldn't think about eating. Her face flushed and she felt heat rise to her cheeks. Just the smell of the food sent Hannah running to the restroom.

"Hannah, are you feeling all right?" Mamm *asked in concern.*

"Ach, nee. Ich feel grank."

"You must be getting the flu. I've heard it's been going around. Go to your room and get some rest. The others can tend to your chores. I'll have Deborah call Fraa Schrock *and tell her you can't make it in to the candle shop today,"* Miriam *insisted.*

"Jah, denki Mamm," Hannah said, while plodding to the *staircase. Each step seemed to drain more and more of her energy. By the time Hannah had made it to her bedroom, she was exhausted. She fell asleep effortlessly, but when she awakened again the nausea returned. And it continued relentlessly over the next week.*

"Hannah, I think you need to go see the doctor. This flu doesn't seem to be going away and all of the color has drained from your face." Miriam worried.

"Nee, Mamm. I'm fine." Hannah attempted to reassure her mother. *"I'm sure I'll get better soon."*

Mamm's *eyes widened as though she'd just had an unimaginable thought. "Hannah, are you...You and Christian haven't entered the marriage bed prematurely, have you?"*

Hannah's cheeks immediately flushed. *"Ach,* nee, Mamm.*"*

"Oh, gut.*" Miriam sighed in relief, placing her hand over her heart. "I'm sorry that I had to ask that. I know you are a* gut dochder. *All right, then. But if you're not better by next week, you will go see the doctor."*

After Mamm *left the room, Hannah placed her hand over her abdomen. Tears filled her eyes. "No. No, please. Dear* Gott, *please don't let me be in the family way. I can't be." But as Hannah silently prayed the words, she realized that they were true. She was pregnant with Samuel Beachy's* boppli.

What would she do now? She couldn't tell Samuel. He was out in Ohio and she'd heard he had already purchased a home for him and Carolanne to move into after they married, which was only a few weeks away. Life had never seemed so hopeless. Hannah knew there was only one solution but it went against everything she'd ever believed; just the thought of it made her weep.

The following week, Mamm *insisted that Hannah get out for some fresh air, convinced that it would help her to feel bet-*

ter. If she only knew, *Hannah thought. She and Deborah had been sent into town to run some errands and the first stop was the fabric shop, which was right next door to a local café. Deborah encouraged her to go in, but Hannah chose to stay in the buggy because she wasn't feeling well.*

Hannah watched as people strolled along the sidewalk, but particularly noticed a group of teen Englisch *girls sitting at one of the umbrella-covered tables outside the café. She was close enough to catch bits and pieces of their conversation and her ears perked up when she heard one word: pregnant. Hannah knew eavesdropping was wrong, but she couldn't help but listen in.*

"I don't know what I'd do if I found out I was pregnant," a blonde girl with a ponytail said. "My parents would so kill me."

Her brunette friend took a sip of her fancy coffee and added, "I know, that would be scary, huh? Poor Brittany, what is she going to do?"

"Well, Erik left and she doesn't have any way to get a hold of him. Besides, he pretty much made it clear that they were through. I think she's seriously considering abortion. She made an appointment with that clinic over on Elm Street for next week."

Deborah hopped back into the buggy just then. "How are you feeling?"

Hannah had to shake her head to pull her thoughts back together. It almost sounded as though the girls had been talking about her, rather than their friend Brittany. "I...I'm okay."

"Is the fresh air helping at all? I think you should go see Danika Yoder and get some herbs. I know they always help me feel better when I'm sick," Deb suggested.

"Jah, maybe I'll do that," Hannah said.

If Deborah only knew that I'm expecting Samuel's baby. What would she think? Would she hate me? Would our relationship be ruined? What would Deborah's beau think of his brother? What would his parents think? *No, like Brittany, she knew there was only one way to get out of this so that no one would know. She couldn't bring shame upon her family, upon Samuel's family, and upon Christian. Hannah determined she would make an appointment at the clinic on Elm Street – the sooner the better.*

Hannah sat in the clinic waiting room alone. She looked down at her Englisch *clothes, or rather, Deborah's* Englisch *clothes. She wore jeans and a red button up short-sleeve top along with a pair of tennis shoes that she had smuggled out of Deb's hope chest. She hoped Deborah wouldn't notice they were missing. Her hair hung in a high ponytail, but she doubled it up so as to make it not appear so long. Today, she wanted to appear authentically* Englisch. *After all, no Amish person would step foot in an abortion clinic – wouldn't even consider it.*

She picked up the clipboard of papers on the plastic seat beside her and signed them as directed. There were so many, she would have been there for hours trying to read and understand them all. The woman at the front desk assured her the forms were routine and that most people don't even bother to read them, so she didn't either. Her hands shook as she signed her name to the papers. She just wanted this whole mess to be over with.

A young couple sat in chairs nearby and she could overhear their conversation.

"I can't do this," the girl cried.

The boy took her hand. "You have to. We don't have any other choice. If your parents find out, you know they'll kick you out of the house. And I'm not ready to be a father."

"What if I decided I want to keep the baby?" Hope filled her eyes.

"Then you can say goodbye to me because I'm not sticking around to help you raise it. I told you I'm too young to have that kind of responsibility. I'll tell everyone that you've been sleeping around and the kid isn't mine."

The girl now sobbed. "You...you would leave me?"

"If that's what I had to do," he said smugly.

Hannah turned away. She couldn't hear any more. What would Samuel do if he were here? Would he be threatening to leave me like this girl's beau is? Would he be encouraging me to get an abortion? *Somehow, she suspected he would be doing the opposite.*

But Samuel wasn't here now. No, he was far away planning a wedding to a woman who probably had no clue about Han-

nah or their relationship. She would not upset Samuel's life. She already knew that he didn't want her or their baby. He'd made that perfectly clear when he left eight weeks ago. Hannah's heart wrenched in pain at the thought of Samuel's rejection. He said he loved me...

Trembling and with tears in her eyes, she followed the worker into a back room. The woman told Hannah that she was making the right decision, a wise decision, but somehow she doubted that was true. If she'd been wise, she would never have given herself to Samuel in the first place. No, she wasn't wise, she was desperate. And no amount of consoling from a stranger would convince her otherwise. She wasn't here because she was choosing to do the best thing; she was here because she felt she had no choice.

Hannah cried out in pain as the procedure began, despite the pain medication they had given her. The dilation process had been painful enough, not to mention embarrassing and shameful. To have a man – a complete stranger – looking upon her and touching her, even if he was a so-called doctor, was utterly humiliating. And by the man's rude bedside manner, she gathered he was only in this profession for the money. She felt worthless, like a piece of discarded trash. Oh, how she wished she was anywhere but here.

Tears flowed from Hannah's eyes when the 'procedure', as they'd called it, was finally over. She had done it. She had ended the life of another, an innocent human being, and she was now a murderer. No matter that the nurse had said they were only removing tissue. Hannah knew the truth. She would spend the rest of her life doing good deeds to make up for this one horrifying act, she knew.

What she thought might bring some relief, only brought more sorrow. Exactly how her life would carry on, she was uncertain. But she took solace in one thing: nobody knew about it. And as long as she never told, nobody would ever know. She could continue on with her life as though it had never happened. Or so she'd thought...

EIGHTEEN

Present day...

Samuel had stayed back at the house while Christian left in the ambulance with Hannah. As he now prepared supper for himself, a knock on the door drew his attention to the side of the *dawdi haus.* He opened up the door to see Christian standing on the small porch with a duffel bag in his hand.

"Christian? How's Hannah doing? Is she all right?" Samuel's brows lowered.

"I'm moving in here with you, Samuel," Christian stated matter-of-factly.

"Why?"

"Hannah is shunned to me now." He stood stock still, his expression stone cold.

"What's going on, Christian?" None of this made any sense to Samuel.

"I no longer have a *fraa.*"

Samuel panicked. "Hannah...she is *dot*?"

"To me, she is."

"Christian, please. You're not making any sense. Where is Hannah?" Samuel asked.

"She is at the hospital," Christian answered.

"What happened? Why do you say she is shunned to you?"

"I cannot say. You must ask the woman," Christian said. "I'm going to sleep now." He walked toward a small bedroom and noticed Samuel's things already occupied the small room. He ambled into the second bedroom and shut the door behind him.

Samuel walked the corridor of the hospital, determined to find out what happened between Hannah and Christian. Like it or not, Hannah was going to have to speak with him. Christian had never been so distressed as to keep his thoughts and feelings bottled up within himself. Samuel had to get to the bottom of this. He would not sit back and watch Christian and Hannah throw their marriage away. Life was too precious to waste it on altercations.

Samuel entered Hannah's room as she wiped away a tear. "Hannah. What happened between you and Christian?"

"I knew it, Samuel. I knew this would happen," Hannah cried shaking her head.

"What are you talking about? What happened?"

"Don't you see, Samuel? All of these things that are happening – you losing Carolanne, me losing my *bopplin*, Christian hating me now – it's what we deserve. God is punishing us for our sin," Hannah said miserably.

Samuel didn't know if Hannah was delirious or not, but finding the answers to why she and Christian were at odds could wait. Her mental and spiritual state were obviously more pressing issues. "Is that what you believe, Hannah? Everything bad that happens in life is because we've done something wrong? That is not how it works, Hannah. When God forgives us, He forgives us fully, unconditionally. The Bible says that He doesn't even remember our sins once they are forgiven. God doesn't hold our sins over our heads and use them to punish us. Jesus took the punishment for us when He shed His blood on the cross," Samuel insisted.

"Then tell me why all these bad things keep happening, Samuel. I want to know. Because surely God could stop them if He wanted to," Hannah spat out bitterly.

"I don't know why, but I do know God can be trusted. Give Him your cares, Hannah. You don't have to bear this burden alone."

Hannah shook her head. "I can't, Samuel. God doesn't listen to me anymore. I know He doesn't love me."

"Hannah, that's not true and you know it."

"Samuel, please. Just leave me alone. I don't want to talk about God anymore. God has failed me."

"Hannah –" Samuel's words cut off when Hannah reached over and flicked the television on with the remote. She turned up the volume to drown out Samuel's unwanted words. Resigned to Hannah's wishes, Samuel left the hospital room. Perhaps he'd be able to talk some sense in to Christian.

Samuel had waited till morning to speak with Christian, hoping a fresh start would mellow out some of the tension of the night before. "Christian, I don't know what's going on between you and Hannah, but you've got to work this out." Samuel and Christian sat at the small table in the *dawdi haus* with mugs of hot morning coffee.

"You don't understand, Samuel. Your *fraa*, she was different than Hannah."

"*Nee*, not so different. She was human; she made mistakes too. We *all* make mistakes," Samuel said.

"No. Not like this," Christian insisted.

"Don't throw your marriage away because of one argument. I'm sure whatever it is, you and Hannah can work this out. Life is too short not to. Trust me on this, I know what I speak of."

"You have no idea what this is about, Samuel. How can you tell me that?" Christian huffed.

"There isn't anything God can't help you through. Seek His Word for guidance. If you don't want to talk to me about it, then confide in Bishop Hostettler or one of the ministers. You have to live with Hannah for the rest of your life," Samuel reasoned.

"Maybe I have to share the same property with her, but I don't have to speak with her. I'll be living in the *dawdi haus* with you now, Samuel. And I'd like you to arrange a ride home from the hospital for Hannah. I don't want to see her." Christian scooted his chair back from the table and emptied the remainder of his coffee in the kitchen sink.

"Christian, I understand that you need time. I will do that for you. But please consider what I have said. I would give just about anything to have another day with Carolanne."

Christian nodded, then went to fetch his hat to begin work for the day.

Hannah hadn't spoken to him the entire trip home. Samuel was at a loss as to what to do, so he silently prayed that Christian and Hannah would work out whatever it was that was causing such heartbreak.

After he helped Hannah down from the buggy, Samuel joined Christian in the field. Christian seemed just as tight-lipped as Hannah, so Samuel did not push the issue. He knew that Christian never could keep his feelings bottled up for long, so he patiently waited until he was ready to speak. Sooner or later he'd share what was on his heart.

"How did you know, Samuel?" Christian said out of the blue.

"How did I know what?" Samuel puzzled.

"How did you know that Carolanne would make a *gut fraa*?"

Samuel thought it odd that Christian would ask such a strange question. He shrugged. "Well, she was kind. She had a good reputation. She was *schee*." Samuel smiled.

"Hannah was all that too. How is it that she's turned out to be a Jezebel?" His face contorted at the words.

A bomb falling from the sky couldn't have shocked Samuel more. "How can you say that, Christian? You have a *gut fraa*."

"You don't know her any better than I thought I did. She is a harlot and a murderer," he said stonily.

Samuel's face sobered. "What are you talking about, Christian?"

"Hannah. She...she had an abortion before we married. The *boppli* was not mine."

Samuel covered his eyes with his hand. "Hannah did? But how? When?"

Christian shrugged. "Ask her."

NINETEEN

So many questions swirled through Samuel's mind as he picked up his pace, heading toward the house. *If Hannah had been pregnant before...*

Samuel stumbled into the kitchen where Hannah sat at the table staring into nothingness. "Was the *boppli* mine?" Samuel blurted out as his heart pounded with emotion. He feared the answer, but realized he needed to hear it just the same.

Hannah remained silent. She never thought this day would come, prayed it would never come. Why couldn't her secret have remained hidden? She had been getting along fine, coping the best way she knew how. Why did this have to come to light? She squeezed her eyes shut, willing Samuel to go away.

"Please, Hannah, I need to know. Was the baby mine?" he pleaded. His heartbeat now thumped in his ears.

Unable to avoid the question any longer, Hannah hung her head in defeat and whispered, *"Jah."*

"Dear *Gott*, no." Samuel didn't attempt to hide his disappointment or mask the anger in his voice. "Why? Why didn't you tell me?" he asked in a shaky voice as tears threatened.

"You said you loved me!" Her accusing stare shot through to his heart.

"I did love you," he insisted.

"Then why did you leave? Why didn't you stay here and marry me? After what we..." Tears choked out her words and she swallowed the lump in her throat. "I thought I meant something to you."

Samuel's eyes held sympathy. He wanted to reach out and pull Hannah close, but he didn't. "Oh, Hannah, you meant a great deal to me. That is partially why I left. I knew that if I stayed here that you and I would have to marry immediately. Because there's no way on this earth, after that night in the barn, that I'd be able to keep my eyes or my hands off of you. Imagine the scandal that would have caused. And Christian, I couldn't do that to him. I couldn't lose his friendship." His words mocked him and he inwardly winced at the irony of it all. "I knew that if I went away, you would eventually go back to Christian. And everything would return to the way it was."

"So you sacrificed me for Christian?"

"*Jah*, in a way, I suppose. But I truly thought you'd be happy with Christian."

"I love Christian; he is a good man. He's been kind and caring...till now."

"Hannah, I wish you would have told me about this. We could have worked something out. Don't you think I had a right to know that you were carrying my *boppli*?" Samuel felt as though a vice had clamped down on his heart and with every word it squeezed tighter.

"I couldn't tell you, Samuel," she whispered in a desperate tone. "You weren't here. You'd left to marry Carolanne."

"But if I'd known, I would have –"

"You would have *what*, Samuel? You would have informed your best friend that his betrothed was in the family way with *your boppli*? Would you have told your beloved Carolanne, 'I'm sorry; we can't get hitched because I fornicated with my best friend's betrothed up in my *vatter*'s haymow'? Or maybe you would have told your folks that you'd brought shame to their respected Beachy name? Don't you see, Samuel? I had no other choice. This seemed like the most logical thing to do."

Logical? Samuel's blood boiled and he raked his hands through his hair in an attempt to calm himself. "Logical? You *kill* my *boppli* and I'm supposed to think it's logical? I was the *vatter*, Hannah! I had a right to know. I could have had a son." His incredulous voice raised an octave. To think his only chance at having a child had been snatched away, stolen without consideration to what *his* desires might be. A lone tear trickled down his cheek. "Did you not think that I may have actually *wanted* my child – our child?" His pained eyes met hers.

"I was all alone. I thought you didn't want me. I was scared, Samuel. What was I supposed to do?" she cried. "I never expected it to turn out this way." Hannah sobbed into her palms. "Oh Samuel, my life is such a mess."

Samuel's anger subsided and he pulled her into his arms, gently stroking her hair. As she wept into his chest, he thought of that night and the tender moments they'd shared. Something that never should have happened. Oh, if he'd only known the outcome of his actions. Things would have turned out so differently. *Surely I would have married Hannah if I'd known about our* boppli. But nothing could erase what they'd done. Nothing could bring their baby back. Choices made, whether bad or good, follow you forever and affect everyone in their path one way or another. "Shh...I'm sorry about my reaction."

"I know now that it was a big mistake. I...I don't know what to do," she cried, clinging to Samuel as though he were her sustenance.

"Christian doesn't have any idea, does he? I mean, that the *boppli* was mine?"

"*Nee*, but he's asked me whose it was. I wouldn't betray you. He has no idea."

Samuel didn't know if he was relieved or disappointed. Surely if Christian found out...*ach*, he hated to think of what the consequences might be. Everything that Samuel had tried to protect – Hannah, his friendship with Christian – had already been, or was on the verge of being destroyed. And there wasn't a single thing he could do about it. "What are we going to do?"

TWENTY

Christian looked up into the blue sky then suddenly stopped in his tracks. The corn stalks gently swayed in the breeze and an unexplainable feeling came over Christian. He glanced at Samuel and noticed…something. He was hiding something. What was it?

"It was you." The barely audible words escaped Christian's lips. But as he said them, he somehow knew deep inside they were true.

"Did you say something?" Samuel must've not heard the words.

"*Jah*, I did. I said it was you. You're the one," Christian said with so little emotion Samuel wondered if he'd just imagined the words.

Samuel knew exactly what he was referring to. *Christian knows?* Samuel's hands began sweating as panic seized his thoughts. *Dear God, what should I do?* There'd already been too many lies, too many secrets. And although Hannah wanted to spare them all grief, it was time the truth be told. "*Jah*, it was me," Samuel admitted shamefully.

What was it in Samuel's eyes? *The look of treachery. The two people I loved and trusted most played me for a fool and betrayed me.* "*Nee.* Please tell me it's not true, Samuel," Christian pled in denial. "Please tell me my closest friend did not..." He couldn't say the words.

Samuel could not look into Christian's eyes. "It was just one time. I'm sorry."

"*You're* sorry?" Sarcasm dripped from Christian's indignant words. "No, I'm the one who's sorry. I'm a sorry fool for thinking I had a loyal friend. I was a *dummkopp* for believing my betrothed – my *fraa* – loved *me.* I'm sorry that the two people I loved and trusted most would be so selfish as to take away my opportunity to see my own offspring. I'm sorry that I've lost three precious *kinner* because of 'just' one night of sin!" Christian's voice shook with fury.

Oh, God. What have I done? Tears filled Samuel's eyes. "Please...forgive me, Christian."

Christian came toe to toe with Samuel and stared him in the eye. "Forgive you? You think a few meaningless words are going to erase everything you've done, everything you've stolen from me? I'd rather go to Hell than forgive you, Samuel Beachy."

"You don't mean that, Christian." Samuel reached out to touch Christian's arm.

Christian quickly shook Samuel's hand off in disgust. "I meant every word. You may leave now. And while you're at it, go ahead and take my *fraa* with you. That's what you came here for in the first place, isn't it? Well, you can have her. She's of no use to me now, but I'm sure she can still provide for your… desires."

"Christian –"

"I said leave *now*! I don't ever want to see your face again."

"You're not being reasonable," Samuel protested.

Christian had had enough. He'd never used violence in his life, had always been taught that it was wrong and went against the ways of his people, but a man could only endure so much. He knew he should walk away, but he didn't. At this moment, not much mattered to him.

His clenched fist met Samuel's face with such force he was immediately knocked to the ground. It felt so good. All his pent-up anger and frustration had finally found its outlet.

As Samuel stumbled back to his feet, blood dripped from his nose. Christian took pleasure in delivering another blow to his stomach, causing Samuel to double over.

Samuel grunted, "Go ahead, Christian. I deserve it."

Christian felt like beating him to a pulp, but instead he took one more disgusted look at his back-stabbing best friend, and then walked away. His life was over. He had nothing now. Such a feeling of grief flooded his soul; he didn't know what to do. In truth, he felt like taking his own life. And he would, if it weren't for the sorrow and shame it would cause his folks.

Christian entered the main house and found Hannah standing near the sink. She was so beautiful, *that Jezebel*, but now he could hardly stand to look at her. "All this time and it was *him*? He's the one you've been covering for all these years? All your depression, all the crying was over *him*?"

Compassion filled Hannah's heart. She could hear the hurt, so evident in his voice. Oh, she'd caused so much pain. "Christian, I–"

"No!" he hollered. "I don't want to hear you're sorry. I'm done, Hannah."

"What are ya sayin'?"

"I'm done with all this. With you. With Samuel. With this whole miserable life." His tired voice trembled.

Christian's pain was unfathomable. Hannah couldn't let him do this to himself; he was such a good man. She knew he was speaking out of grief. She went to him, but he brushed her aside and turned back toward the door he'd just entered. "Please don't leave, Christian. I don't know what I'd do without you," she said in desperation.

"Oh, I see. So *now* you want me?"

"I've always wanted you!" she cried.

"*Nee*, not always." His accusing stare bore through her.

She wanted to scream at him and tell him this was all his fault. If he hadn't cheated on her with that stupid *Englisch* girl, she wouldn't have been in Samuel's arms. She wouldn't have gotten pregnant. And she wouldn't have killed an innocent human life. They would have their own *kinner* – alive, healthy and happy. But she didn't say anything. She realized that she alone bore the guilt and shame of what she'd done. And all the excuses in the world couldn't have justified it.

"Christian, we never intended to…it just happened. What Samuel and I did, it was a mistake," she said miserably.

"No, I'm the one that made the mistake. I never should have trusted you. I never should have married you."

Hannah desperately wanted to draw him into her arms and hold him tight, to give him comfort and reassurance. She craved for him to pull her close and tell her that she was forgiven and they could work this out, but she realized now that would never happen. Her sin truly was unforgivable. "You don't mean that, Christian! I know you love me," she wailed.

"*Nee*, not anymore, Hannah." Christian strengthened his resolve. "This is my house and I don't want you here any longer. I can't stand the sight of you anymore. Go pack your things and leave," he ordered.

This couldn't be happening. "No, Christian."

Anger rose up inside him and he pounded his fist on the table, knocking over the Mason jar that held flowers from Hannah's garden. "Don't tell me no! I said get out."

Trembling, Hannah ran to their bedroom, threw herself across their bed, and wept once again. How could she have messed up her life so badly? How could one mistake snowball into such an avalanche that she had no idea how to get out from under it?

After a few minutes, she arose from the bed and found the only suitcase she owned. As she began removing items from her hope chest and bureau, tears streamed down her cheeks and her shoulders heaved. Hannah never imagined she could cause so much pain. She did not want to lose Christian; she'd already lost so much. If she left right now, she didn't know how any of them would move on with their lives.

"I'm sorry about all this, Hannah," Samuel's voice sounded from the doorway.

Hannah looked up at him, surprised that Christian had allowed him into the house.

Samuel sensed her apprehension. "Don't worry. Christian is not here. He took off in the buggy," he explained.

"*Ach*, Samuel, your face." She looked on his bruised and bloodied face with empathy.

"Don't worry about it. I deserved much worse than what I got."

"I don't know what I'm going to do," Hannah said, wiping away a fresh wave of tears. "Christian doesn't want me anymore."

Samuel approached and placed a gentle hand on her shoulder. "Come with me, Hannah. You may not believe this, but I do love you."

"But what about Christian?" she protested. "I can't leave him."

"Didn't you just say he won't have you anymore? He *told* me to take you with me. I'm sorry, Hannah, but I'm quite certain your marriage is over. I don't think Christian will ever forgive us," Samuel said dejectedly. "I promise I'll take care of you. We can start again and build a new life together."

"But we're Amish, Samuel. I can't get a...a..." she struggled to say the word, virtually unheard of in their culture, "... divorce," she contended.

"*Nee*, Hannah. You and I, we can no longer be Amish. No Amish district will accept us now. What we have done, it's unforgivable." Samuel clarified. "They would say that we are forgiven, *jah*, but in their hearts we would still be outcasts. Nobody would want to have anything to do with us. We must become *Englischers*. There is no other way."

"I don't know how to live in the *Englisch* world, Samuel. The Amish life is all I've ever known," she said. "And my family, how can I leave them?"

"Do you think your family will accept you now?"

"You are right. I know they could not accept me. I've brought so much shame," Hannah cried.

Samuel comforted Hannah, pulling her close. "I will take care of you, Hannah. I promise. We will get through this together."

"But I still love Christian."

"Of course you do. You will always love Christian. Nothing will ever change that." Samuel sighed and brushed away her tears. His sincere eyes looked into hers. "I'm so sorry, Hannah. I've failed you in so many ways."

"We've both failed, Samuel."

"Give me a chance to make it up to you. I know we'll never get our *boppli* back. And part of us will always be broken. It won't be easy, but you won't have to do it alone," Samuel pledged.

Hannah sniffled, drawing strength from Samuel's comfort. "*Denki*, Samuel. I don't know what I'd do without you. You are all I have left."

Samuel's hands cradled her soft face and he gazed into her troubled eyes. He bent down and gently brushed his lips to hers. "I love you, Hannah," he whispered.

Neither one of them heard the buggy rumble up the driveway. Nor did either of them hear Christian enter the house. But there he was, irate, and standing in the doorway. "How dare you! Could you not even wait to get her alone in a hotel room, Samuel? Must you take my *fraa* in my own house? Before my very eyes?" Christian clenched his hands, struggling to keep his composure. "I'm going to the barn to unhitch Cowboy. When I get back, you'd better both be gone. And I don't ever want to see you again!" He aimed one last penetrating glare at Hannah and then trudged out the back door.

Inside the barn, Christian stumbled onto a bale of hay. "Why God? Why? I don't understand." As he sat in the darkness with his face in his hands, tears flowed freely from his eyes. It was unquestionable in his mind whether there was any pain on this earth worse than what he now suffered. He'd rarely cried as a man, and as he now wept, he realized he didn't possess the strength he thought he had. Never in his life could he have ever imagined experiencing such excruciating heartache.

The sound of buggy wheels and gentle trotting drove another dagger through his heart. Everything he loved most in this life was now driving away in that buggy. When the echo of hoof beats had faded into nothingness, Christian stood, his feeble knees barely holding the weight of his one hundred and eighty pound frame. He slowly ambled toward the house, hoping it would bring some sense of solace. Instead, it was cold and empty. Exactly how he felt.

He realized he needed strength, sustenance that couldn't come from bread alone. He desperately needed God.

Christian entered his bedroom to retrieve his Bible from the top drawer of his desk. He glanced at the bed – his and Hannah's marriage bed – a place meant to be kept sacred and undefiled. *How many times had she been thinking of Samuel instead of me when we'd lain together?* The disgusting thought sickened him to his stomach.

With a detached rage, Christian began opening all the drawers in Hannah's dresser. He threw out everything she had left in them until they were completely empty. Likewise, he did the same with what was left in her hope chest. Lifting out a delicate tea cup, Hannah's favorite, he threw it against the wall, shattering it into thousands of tiny pieces. A perfect symbol of his life.

He grabbed his clothing and Bible and stomped into the spare bedroom. If he could help it, he would never step foot into that room again.

TWENTY-ONE

*D*eborah sat next to Peter in their buggy as they traveled back home from the hospital. She was thankful that her mother had agreed to watch the *kinner* while they went to see Hannah. They were surprised that she'd been released so soon, and even more surprised that Christian hadn't told them. Of course, she knew Hannah didn't care much for hospitals and would have been longing for home.

Deb was astonished when *Mamm* said that Hannah'd had another miscarriage. Deborah could usually detect when her sister was in the family way, but it seemed she'd been able to conceal this pregnancy well. Deborah's heart ached for Hannah. To have been in the family way three times and still have no *boppli* to hold must be hard. Deborah felt somewhat guilty that she had two healthy *kinner*, and Hannah still had none. And now that she was expecting again, she was hesitant to tell Hannah, especially in light of another miscarriage.

The shrill of an ambulance in the distance sent chills up Deborah's spine. Ever since she'd been a child, she'd hated that sound. It had always been a symbol of sadness and pain. Somebody's someone was in that ambulance and somebody's heart was breaking. As she always did, she sent up a quick prayer for whomever was in distress at the moment.

The traffic ahead of them seemed to be going even slower than their horse. Deborah tried to stand up a bit to see around the vehicle in front of her, but Peter quickly pulled her back into the seat. He'd always been overprotective.

"*Ach*, what do you think is happening up there?" Deborah asked.

"I don't know," Peter yelled, as two screaming ambulances passed their buggy heading in the opposite direction. "Must've been an accident of some kind."

Deborah anxiously waited as the traffic inched forward at painstakingly slow speeds. She couldn't imagine how impatient the *Englisch* drivers in their fast automobiles must be. After another twenty minutes, she could finally see where a police officer stood waving traffic through. When they reached the officer, he asked them to pull off to the side of the road.

"Excuse me, Sir, but yours is the first Amish buggy to drive by. I was hoping you could possibly help us identify the driver of the buggy that was in the accident," the officer requested.

"*Jah*, I will see if I know who it is." Peter descended the carriage. "Deborah, why don't you stay here?"

Deborah nodded, not sure her stomach would be able to handle seeing wreckage. She watched as Peter walked across the street with the officer. Up ahead, a mangled buggy, turned over on its side, littered the road's shoulder with a detached buggy wheel fifty feet away. *Dear God, please let the people be okay. Please don't let it be anybody we know,* she prayed quietly while keeping an eye on Peter.

Peter and the officer crouched down next to a long white sheet. As the officer lifted the sheet, Deborah saw her husband immediately look away. When he looked back at the body under the sheet, his hands went to his face and he bowed his head. *Oh no! He knows who it is.* Deborah couldn't stand being in the buggy a moment longer. She hopped down and raced across the street.

"Peter, who is it?" she asked fearfully.

Peter looked up. Tears glistened in his eyes. "My *bruder.*"

She glanced at the covered stretcher whereby Peter crouched. "Samuel? He...he is gone?"

The officer spoke up. "I'm afraid so, Ma'am. The woman that was with him – his wife – I assume, was taken to the hospital. She was unconscious."

"Wife? Oh no, Peter. Do you think it could be Hannah?" Deborah asked helplessly. She glanced around, taking in the wreckage. Her eyes widened when they landed on something she recognized: Hannah's suitcase. "It *is* Hannah, Peter. We have to go."

Peter looked up at Deborah with pained eyes. "My *bruder...*"

"It's all right, Sir. We will take care of him. Just have one of your people stop by the station. When the funeral arrangements are made, we can deliver the body. I will need his full name for identification purposes," the officer said.

"Samuel. Samuel Beachy of Paradise. Bishop Hostettler's district," he stated evenly. "My *vatter* will come in to get Samuel. We – our people – will prepare his body."

"Very well. Here is my card if you need to contact me." The officer rubbed his chin. "You folks need a ride to the hospital?"

"*Nee,*" Peter said. "We will take our buggy."

"All right. Be safe, then."

Deborah and Peter hastily walked into the hospital in search of Hannah. It was difficult to believe she'd just been there earlier in the day to see Hannah and now she was back again. When Deborah noticed nobody in attendance at the information desk, she was ready to pull her hair out. She impatiently rang the brass bell on top of the counter. Peter's comforting hand rubbed her back although she knew he was still in shock from learning of Samuel's death. She rang the bell again and when nobody answered they set out to find a nurses' station.

As their feet pounded the corridor, Deborah's mind whirled. *Where were Samuel and Hannah going? Where was Christian? Why did Hannah have her suitcase with her?* Then another thought occurred to her. *Were Samuel and Hannah running off together?* To Deborah, the thought seemed preposterous. She had warned Hannah about Samuel living with them, but she never thought that they would do something like that. Samuel and Hannah were both levelheaded and responsible. Deborah couldn't imagine the two of them doing anything of the sort, it was simply uncharacteristic.

Deborah was shaken from her thoughts when they arrived at the nurses' station. "My sister, Hannah Glick, she was in an accident not too long ago," Deborah uttered.

"You'll need to exit this building and enter the emergency wing on the south side of Building A. She's in ICU right now, but I don't have any details. Chances are, you won't be able to see her for a while if she was recently admitted," a plump woman with graying hair and hot pink spectacles advised.

"Thank you." Deborah turned to go.

"Uh, if you want I can call and try to get a little more information before you walk all the way over there. I'd hate to have you go all that way just to find out that you can't see her," the friendly nurse said.

"*Denki*, we would appreciate that," Peter spoke.

The woman advised them to take a seat while she picked up the telephone and dialed a number. A moment later she called them back over to the window. "She is in surgery now and probably won't be out till late tonight. She'll be under anesthesia so you most likely won't be able to get in to see her until tomorrow."

Deborah looked at Peter and frowned. She stepped up to the window to speak with the nurse once again. "What is Hannah having surgery for? Is my sister going to be okay?"

"I'm not certain, Dear. I'm sorry I don't have more information for you. You may call back in the morning to check whether they will be allowing visitors or not."

"Thank you. We will return tomorrow," Peter said, gently grasping Deborah's elbow. "Let's go, Deborah. We must tell *Dat* and *Mamm* about Samuel. And Christian and your folks will want to know about Hannah, I'm sure."

Deborah didn't put up a fight, given the situation with Samuel's family. Besides, she was anxious to talk to Christian about Hannah and set her mind at ease as to why Samuel and her sister were riding alone in Samuel's buggy.

After breaking the heart-wrenching news about Samuel to Peter's folks, Deborah's head was still filled with unanswered questions. While Samuel's parents knew Hannah was involved in the accident, nobody dared bring up the fact that she and Samuel had been riding together alone. Peter was at a loss as well, and since his brother was now gone, Deborah determined not to worry him further with her speculations. Only two people held the answers to her questions: Hannah, who was incapacitated at the moment and in no condition to be interrogated, and Christian.

When Deborah and Peter arrived at the Glick farm, they'd first walked out to the field expecting Christian to be working. After determining he wasn't there, they checked the barn to no avail, then finally decided to try the house. They knocked on the door twice, but Christian did not open it.

Deborah frowned at her husband. "Do you suppose something is wrong?"

"He should be here. His carriage is in the barn," Peter said.

"Let's just go in," Deborah said, pushing the door open before Peter had a chance to object.

The house seemed quiet – too quiet. Something wasn't right. Deborah rushed to Hannah's and Christian's bedroom and gasped when she saw Hannah's things strewn everywhere. Her eyes widened when she saw Hannah's teacup shattered in pieces on the floor.

"This doesn't look too good, Deb," Peter commented behind her.

"Peter, what do you think happened? You don't suppose Hannah and Christian had a fight?"

A noise drew their attention down the hallway. They quickly but cautiously walked to where they'd heard the sound. Peter gingerly opened the door to the spare bedroom where Christian sat on the floor near the bed with his head in his hands.

"Christian, are you all right?" Peter asked.

Christian looked up with bleary red-rimmed eyes, his face contorted with pain. "They're gone." His bottom lip trembled as he said the words.

Never in her life had Deborah seen Christian in such a state. He'd always been calm and confident, even when Hannah had her troubles. "What happened?"

"Your sister and his brother left together. The last I saw of them they were kissing in our bedroom." Christian's disgusted tone evidenced his bitterness. "I'm through with both of them." That explained the disaster in the bedroom.

Hannah was kissing Samuel? Oh no. Deborah couldn't imagine it. *Lord, please tell me they weren't committing adultery this whole time.*

"Christian, Hannah and Samuel were in an accident. Samuel...he is gone. Hannah is in intensive care at the hospital," Peter said.

Christian eyed them both wearily. Indifferent, he shrugged. "So be it."

Enraged, Deborah raised her voice, "Don't you even care that your best friend is dead? That your *fraa* is in the hospital? She could die, Christian."

"I don't have a *fraa* anymore. She is already dead to me."

Peter and Deborah looked at each other helplessly. It was clear that they weren't going to be able to get through to Christian, especially in his current state. They would need to consult with the bishop and see if he'd be willing to console Christian. And as soon as Hannah was able, Deborah was going to have a talk with her older sister to find out what exactly happened. She refused to believe that Hannah would have an immoral relationship with another man – *any* man – while she was married to Christian. Surely there must be some logical explanation.

TWENTY-TWO

*D*eborah had tossed and turned all night. She might as well have stayed at the hospital since she wasn't going to get any sleep anyway. Of course she hadn't known that beforehand, but she should have figured. After visiting Christian last night, she and Peter had informed her parents about the accident. *Mamm* was presently at the hospital waiting for Hannah to awaken.

She hadn't told her folks about Christian's state of mind or what he'd said about Hannah and Samuel. Deborah knew she should first talk to Hannah and find out what actually happened between her, Samuel, and Christian. If what Christian said was indeed true, she couldn't blame him for being upset.

Peter agreed to go and talk with the bishop today. They'd been too exhausted, both physically and emotionally, to visit him last night. Deborah also realized that Peter needed time to grieve his brother's death. She couldn't imagine what it would be like losing one of her sisters, especially Hannah. Samuel and

Peter had been pretty close in the past, so she knew he must be reeling inside although superficially he appeared strong.

As Deborah now entered Hannah's hospital room, she shared a sympathetic look with *Mamm,* who'd been sitting at Hannah's bedside. *Mamm* quietly motioned her out into the hallway.

"I'm worried about her, Deb. She's been awake for two hours now and hasn't said more than two words to me," Miriam said anxiously.

"What has she heard about the accident? Does she know about Samuel?" Deborah asked cautiously, not wanting to give too much away.

"She knows she was in a buggy accident, but has no idea about Samuel. It wonders me if she fully understands what happened. The doctors have her on pain medication, so that might have her a bit *ferhoodled.*"

"*Jah,* perhaps. *Mamm,* would you mind if I have some time alone with Hannah?" Deborah asked.

"*Nee.* I've been dying to go downstairs to the cafeteria, but I didn't want to leave Hannah's side. The doctors said that she'd be able to go home at the end of the week. Other than a slight concussion, a broken arm, and a few stitches, I'd say Hannah escaped pretty well," Miriam said.

"*Gott* must have been looking out for her," Deborah agreed.

Miriam Stolzfus left Deborah and headed down the hallway. Deborah took a deep breath, said a quick prayer, and then entered Hannah's room. Hannah didn't bother to turn her head when she came in, but instead stared at the wall in front of her. She appeared sallow and disheartened. Deborah debated whether to share the news of Samuel or not.

"Han, how are you doing?" Deb reached out and touched her sister's arm.

Hannah glanced at Deborah, then a lone tear trickled down her cheek.

Deborah walked over to Hannah and gave her an awkward hug, trying not to jostle her broken arm. "Shh...it'll be all right, Hannah," she said, attempting to comfort her sister.

"Samuel? Where...where is he, Deborah?"

Like it or not, she was going to have to be honest with Hannah. She gave her sister a sympathetic look and her own eyes filled with tears. "I'm sorry, Hannah. Samuel is gone. *Der Herr* took him home."

"He...he is *dot*? No!" Hannah shook her head. "He can't do that to me, Deborah. Haven't I paid enough for my sin already? Why did He have to take Samuel too? He was all I had left," Hannah cried. "I wish He'd taken me. Why won't He let me die too?"

"What do you mean? What sin are you paying for? I don't understand, Hannah. Help me understand," Deb pleaded.

"I killed Samuel's baby, Deborah," Hannah cried miserably.

Deborah figured the medication Hannah was taking must be confusing her thoughts. "What do you mean? Samuel didn't have any children."

Hannah shook her head adamantly. "Nobody knew about it. When Samuel left for Ohio, I was expecting his *boppli*. That's why I was so sick. I was scared, Deborah. I thought Samuel didn't love me. I didn't know what to do, so I went to the clinic and..." Her voice trailed off, giving way to sobs.

"You were in the family way at eighteen?" Deborah couldn't believe the words she was hearing. How could Hannah, *perfect* Hannah, have gotten pregnant? And with Samuel's baby nonetheless. "Samuel didn't know?"

Hannah found her voice. "At the time, no. He found out yesterday."

"And what about Christian?"

"He found out too." Hannah brushed away another tear. "The doctor said that's the reason I keep losing *bopplin*. He said my cervix had been damaged during the procedure and had been preventing me from carrying the babies to term. Deborah, I can't ever have a *boppli* now. My life is ruined. Christian doesn't love me anymore. Now Samuel is gone forever. And I know as soon as everyone else finds out, they will despise me too. Why do I have to live, Deborah? I don't understand. Why won't God kill *me*? I just want to die."

Tears streamed from Deborah's eyes as she pulled her sister close and held her tight. She couldn't fathom the emotional pain and guilt Hannah must be experiencing. No wonder her sister had been so depressed all the time. To have carried this secret around all those years must've been excruciating. And then to blame herself for everything bad that's happened since then. Deborah realized that her sister needed more help than what she could offer, but she attempted to console her anyway.

"No, Hannah. Please don't say that. We don't want you to die. We love you. You were young and desperate and you made a mistake. We all make mistakes, Hannah. All these things that have happened are not your fault. And regardless of how you may feel, God still loves you."

"I can't do it anymore, Deborah. I can't go on." Hannah's hopelessness gripped Deborah's heart.

Deborah realized that she was not going to be able to penetrate the darkness that surrounded Hannah's soul. She desperately needed help, professional spiritual help from someone who could relate to her circumstances. But Deborah had never personally known of anyone that had gone through an abortion. It wasn't exactly something that people shouted from the rooftops. No, Deborah suspected that there were probably many more women in Hannah's shoes than she realized. How many people – did she cross on a daily basis – carried around the silent pain of a secret abortion?

TWENTY-THREE

*D*etermined to complete the last few rows by night fall, Christian urged the team of draft horses forward. Sweat dripped from his brow, evidencing the hours he'd been in the field. As the team turned another loop, Christian spied a carriage coming up the lane. He squinted to see who might have come to call. It appeared to be Minister Fisher's buggy.

Great, that's all I need. Christian grimaced.

He continued to work as though he hadn't noticed the minister. *Maybe if I keep working, he'll go away.* Christian advanced onward while puffs of dust rose into the air. He'd completed more work than he remembered ever doing in one day. It would have felt good if it weren't for the fact that he couldn't get Hannah off his mind. He didn't want to care for her, but he still did. As upset as he was about what she and Samuel had done, he knew he still loved her. He would always consider her the love of his life. But there was no way he was going to forgive her.

"*Hullo*, Christian." Minister Fisher's voice called out. The minister stood at the end of the row now, just a few feet ahead of the team.

Christian brought the horses to an abrupt stop in order to avoid running the minister over. "Are you *ab im kopp*?"

Minister Fisher's blue eyes sparkled. "It's been said."

"I could have killed you."

The minister shrugged. "I'm still here, aren't I? The fact that you brought that team to a stop proves that you're a good man, Christian."

"There is none good."

"Ah, I see you've been reading the Scriptures. Or perhaps paying attention at meeting."

"Look, Minister Fisher –"

"Jonathan. Just Jonathan."

"Look, Jonathan. I've got work to do here. I intend to finish this field tonight."

"I need to speak with you on some important matters."

"I ain't got time for talking," Christian insisted.

"Go ahead and finish up. I can wait. I'll just go up to the house and put some coffee on for us." Jonathan turned to go.

Christian remembered the mess in the bedroom. "Uh, on second thought, would you mind helping me unhitch the team? I think I'll call it a day."

Jonathan hid a smirk. "Sure."

Christian set two mugs of hot coffee on the table. "You like cream and sugar?"

Jonathan nodded silently.

Christian placed the cream and sugar on the table then watched as Minister Fisher lumped five heaping spoons of sugar into his mug. "Does your *fraa* let you put that much sugar in your coffee?" He knew Hannah would've protested if he'd tried to do the same thing.

"Na. I just take it when Susie's not looking." Jonathan smiled mischievously. "Sometimes the *kinner* tell on me, though."

"So what happens when you get caught?"

"She comes and kisses me and tells me I'm already sweet enough." His eyes sparkled.

If only Hannah and I had that kind of relationship. Christian sighed. Who knows? Perhaps he could learn a thing or two from the minister. "You wanted to speak with me about something?"

"Why are you not with your *fraa* at the hospital?"

Christian did not expect such a direct question. "She is shunned to me."

"How do you figure that?" Jonathan's eyebrows rose.

"My *fraa* is a Jezebel. She fornicated with Samuel Beachy before we got hitched then killed their unborn *boppli*. I just found all this out a couple of days ago." He scowled.

"I see." Jonathan scratched his beard. "So she has not asked for forgiveness?"

"She has."

"Yet you choose not to forgive?"

"How can a person forgive something like that, Jonathan?" Christian's voice rose. "If it were your *fraa,* would you forgive her?"

"It would be difficult, but *jah,* I would. We must follow Christ's example. Do you think it was easy for Him to forgive those who nailed Him to the cross?"

"*Nee.* But I am not Christ. He was perfect." Christian took a sip of his coffee.

"Perfect, *jah.* But a man, like us. It wasn't any easier for Him." Jonathan tapped the table. "Have you considered the prophet Hosea?"

Christian's eyebrows furrowed. *Which prophet was he?* He strove to remember but came up blank. "I don't know if I remember which one that is."

"*Jah,* all those prophets are sometimes hard to keep straight." Jonathan chuckled. "He was the one whom God told to marry a harlot."

Christian still couldn't recall that story. "God told someone to get hitched to a harlot?"

"Yep. Think I would've had a hard time obeying that one."

"Why would God tell him to do that?" Christian wondered.

"To show His people how much he loved them. You see, no matter how much God's people messed up, He always forgave them when they turned back to Him. It was a picture of His unconditional love." Jonathan went on. "Unconditional love is not human. We can only give it by the strength that comes from *Der Herr.*"

Christian pondered the minister's words. He realized he hadn't been forgiving at all. No, he'd been judgmental, hateful, and vengeful. "Samuel had asked for forgiveness, but I did not grant it. Now, it's too late. I'll never have another chance to make amends with Samuel. My best friend died thinking I hated him." The thought now brought tears to his eyes.

Jonathan listened quietly, allowing Christian to unburden himself.

"My *fraa* lies in the hospital probably thinking the same thing." He thought of Hannah and all the *kinner* they'd lost. Next, she'd been rejected by Christian. And now, she'd lost Samuel. He couldn't imagine the emotional grief she must be experiencing. His heart ached just thinking about it. "I will go to her."

"Perhaps you should spend some time in prayer first," Jonathan suggested.

Christian nodded. "*Jah*, that is a *gut* idea. I will do that."

"I'd like to pray with you before I leave."

"*Denki*, Jonathan. You don't know how much I appreciate you coming by today." He hung his head. "I'm ashamed to say that I didn't want you here at first."

"I know." Minister Fisher smiled as they bowed their heads in prayer.

TWENTY-FOUR

*D*eborah whisked a dozen eggs in a plastic mixing bowl, then dumped them into the hot pan to scramble. The table was already set, so she only needed to butter the bread now and put it in the oven to toast. Peter sat at the table reading his Bible with Elam on his lap, while Becky still slept in her crib. Deborah never realized how blessed she truly was, nor how oblivious to those around her in pain.

Like Hannah. How could it be that Hannah had suffered in silence this long and Deborah not have noticed? She'd failed as a sister and a friend. She should have been able to discern Hannah's anguish, shouldn't she?

Now that she thought back on everything that had happened over the years, it all made perfect sense. Beginning with the day Hannah'd found out that Christian cheated on her with the *Englisch* girl, she hadn't been the same. Deborah gasped at the realization. *It was Christian who caused Hannah and Samuel to come together,* she was almost sure of it. What else could it have been? *This is all Christian's fault!*

Deborah clenched her hands together. *Ugh...the nerve of that man!* In her frustration, she nearly knocked over one of the glasses she'd set on the table.

Peter's eyes lifted. "Are you all right, Deborah?"

"No, I am not all right. I'm upset. I'm angry. I'm furious!"

Peter set his Bible down and peered into Deborah's eyes. "Whoa! Calm down there. What's this all about?"

"Him." She clenched her teeth.

"Him? Him who? Samuel?" Peter said, thinking she looked cute when she was angry.

"*Nee.*"

"Christian?"

Deborah nodded her head.

Peter set Elam down on the bench. "Well, if what you said about Hannah was true, don't you think he had a right to be upset?"

"That's not what I'm talking about, Peter. Don't you see? This is all Christian's fault, every bit of it. It's all because he cheated on Hannah when they were betrothed. *He's* the reason she turned to your brother."

"Deb, I know what you're saying. But Hannah and Samuel are not innocent in this. They still made a choice to do what they did. They chose to sin. Hannah chose to abort their baby. Let's not go blaming people and just let God take care of this, *jah*?" Peter pulled Deborah into his arms and soothingly rubbed her back.

Deborah released a drawn out breath. "Okay, I'll try. But I still feel like wringing Christian's neck."

Peter chuckled. "Wow. I never knew my *fraa* could be so violent. Maybe I should watch my back."

"*Nee*, you don't need to do that. Unless you make me mad," she warned.

Peter bent down and brought his lips to hers. "I would never want to do that," he said, enjoying his wife's nearness.

Deborah suddenly pulled away. "I have an idea! I think I know how we can help Hannah and Christian. Do you remember that billboard on Lincoln Highway – the one with the mother and baby on it?"

Peter sighed in disappointment and stepped back, shaking his head to refocus. "*Jah*, I remember."

"Well, I think those people help women who've been through abortion. Could we drive by and get the phone number?" Deborah watched as Peter's longing eyes swept over her dress. She had a feeling he hadn't heard a word she'd said.

"I think we can do that later," Peter mumbled. He stepped close to Deborah and drew her back into his arms. "Right now I need some time with my *fraa*."

Deborah flustered. "But breakfast is ready now," she protested.

"Breakfast can wait." His eyes twinkled as his fingers caressed her soft cheek.

"But the kinner –" She glanced around to where Elam was sitting and noticed he'd gone to play with his toys in the other room.

"Are occupied." He kissed his wife again, then scooped her up into his arms.

Hannah awoke when her mother entered her hospital room. Loneliness and despair were like a continual plague that ceased to lift. Sleep was the only luxury she'd allow. If not for the intravenous fluid, she'd receive no nourishment at all.

Miriam Stolzfus frowned when she noticed the dark circles under her daughter's eyes. "Hannah, *dochder,* it breaks my heart to see you like this. Please talk to me. Tell me why you're so down."

Deborah hasn't told Mamm *yet.* Hannah didn't know whether she was relieved or disappointed. *What would* Mamm *say if she knew I killed her* grossboppli? *The only* boppli *I could have given birth to. Surely she'd hate me.* Hannah remained silent. She couldn't bear any more shame.

Hannah heard the door to her room swing open, but the privacy curtain blocked her view. She saw *Mamm* look up at the visitor with sad eyes and give a half smile. *Mamm* looked back at her. "I'll be back later, Honey."

After *Mamm* disappeared, quiet footsteps neared Hannah's bed. Hannah glanced up, surprised to see a hesitant Christian.

She quickly looked away, fearful of what he'd say to her. Why was he here anyway? Hadn't he told her to leave and that he never wanted to see her again? He almost got his wish. He had with Samuel.

Christian sucked in a breath. *Hannah.* Precious Hannah. Oh, he'd come so close to losing her. *God, give me the strength to love her like You do. Help me to see past her faults. Place Your love and forgiveness in my heart and help us to overcome this trial.*

"Hannah." Christian began slowly. He cautiously walked toward her. Summoning the courage to lift his eyes, he saw that she did not look his way. "I've come to apologize. I was wrong. Please forgive me for being a *dummkopp.*"

Hannah turned and lifted her sad eyes to his. "You...you don't hate me?"

Tears sprung to his eyes. "*Nee.* I could never hate you, *Lieb.*" He took her uninjured hand in his and gently brought it to his lips. He sat in the chair near her bed.

"But Samuel..." Hannah's voice trailed off.

"All is forgiven." Tears now streamed from Christian's eyes and he brushed them away. "We've lost him, Hannah. We've lost Samuel forever."

Hannah swiped her eyes too. "*Nee*, not forever."

"We will miss him, *jah?*" Christian held out his arms and Hannah wept in his embrace. As they both mourned Samuel's death, he realized how good it felt to hold her in his arms again. Four days had seemed like an eternity without her. But he knew everything would be okay now.

Hannah pulled back and peered into his eyes. "Samuel did this."

Christian didn't comprehend what she was saying. "Samuel did what?"

"When Samuel went away to Ohio, he said he'd done it so we could be together. He never meant to come between us. The last thing he said to me before the accident was, 'Hannah, I would go away and never come back if I thought it would heal your and Christian's marriage.' Do you think God answered his unspoken prayer? Do you think Samuel gave up his life for us?" Hannah's eyes glistened.

"It would seem that way." Christian contemplated his friendship with Samuel. But something nagged at him. He'd always seemed like such a faithful, caring friend, so why would he betray his trust? Why would he have gotten involved with Hannah?

"Hannah, I have to ask you something." Christian receded from their embrace.

Hannah nodded, giving him permission to speak.

"Why did you turn to Samuel in the first place?" He needed to know, if he was ever going to have peace.

"Do you remember the night of the Singing? After I'd seen you with the *Englisch* girl and we argued?"

He nodded and gulped.

"That was the night I turned to Samuel." Tears sprung to her eyes once again as she remembered that agonizing night. "I was so upset, so hurt that you'd chosen an *Englisch* girl over me. I thought we'd never marry. Samuel was there for me. He cared and he told me that he loved me. But then when Samuel left..." She couldn't go on. The memories were just too vivid, and too painful.

Christian swore under his breath, something Hannah had never heard him do. "It was all my fault." Christian shook his head at the realization. "I'm the one who –"

"Christian, no. Don't blame yourself. Samuel and I –"

"Hannah, forgive me. I had no idea. I thought..." Christian raked his hands through his hair, thoroughly humbled. "I'm just as much to blame for all this as you and Samuel. I'm so sorry, Hannah."

"I love you, Christian."

"Oh, *Lieb*. Why did God ever see fit to bless me with a woman like you? I'm so undeserving." Christian met her lips with his and he realized for the first time just how truly blessed he was.

TWENTY-FIVE

A long line of gray buggies somberly made their way out to the Amish cemetery where generations of their Anabaptist ancestors had been buried. Today marked a grievous day for Bishop Hostettler's district in Paradise, Pennsylvania. They would be saying goodbye to one of their younger members, Samuel Beachy.

Christian and Hannah followed the procession to bid farewell to their beloved friend. Samuel would be missed immensely. They hadn't been to the Beachy home to view the body prior to the graveside service because Hannah hadn't been released from the hospital yet. She'd pleaded with the doctor to allow an early release for the funeral.

Christian helped Hannah down from the carriage, careful not to jostle her broken arm. Her injury would be a constant reminder of that fateful day. But as her broken body healed, her aching heart would eventually heal as well.

Hundreds of mourners, all dressed in black, slowly made their way to the hollow earth where Samuel's body would be laid to rest. Hannah caught the glances from others who pretended not to notice her. Would they look at her and wonder what she'd been doing in Samuel's buggy? Did they believe she was responsible for his death? Did they wish that it was she who had died instead of Samuel? Had word already gotten out about her and Samuel's misdeed? Or worse, did they know she was a murderer?

As Hannah furtively glanced around, she spotted her mother. *Mamm* still hadn't asked about it and she wondered how long it would be before she did. Hannah's heart lamented every time she thought of telling her folks. How could she tell them she'd killed their *grossboppli*? They would never have expected such an atrocious act of *her*. No, she'd always been the 'good' daughter – an example for her younger sister to follow. *Yeah right.* The only thing she exemplified was how to make a complete disaster of one's life.

While Christian moved in closer, Hannah opted to stay back. She wasn't quite ready to face the crowds and worried that her arm might get bumped. Deborah came near and slipped an arm around her. Her sister's presence was comforting. Somehow it seemed as though they had reversed roles over the years.

Deborah leaned close and spoke softly, so no one but Hannah would hear. "Samuel's in Heaven with his *boppli* now, *jah*?"

The words were like a soothing balm to Hannah's aching soul. "*Jah.*" *Denki, Gott.* Hannah closed her eyes and pictured Samuel holding their baby with Jesus standing by his side. She'd never seen Samuel happier. The beautiful vision provoked a fresh wave of cleansing tears.

As the final words were said and the pine box was lowered into the ground, Hannah felt an overwhelming peace flood her soul. *Samuel is home*, she realized.

It felt good to be back home. Hannah prepared coffee and a light snack for Christian and herself while they enjoyed the quiet evening in each other's company. Attending Samuel's funeral had been difficult, but she realized it was a necessary step in finding closure. They would miss Samuel immensely and she knew he would never be forgotten.

Hannah brought a mug of coffee into the living room and handed it to Christian. "How are you doing?" she asked.

Christian's glazed eyes met hers. He shrugged. "All right, I guess. I will miss him."

Hannah glanced down and spied an envelope in his lap on top of his open Bible. "What's that you got there?"

He picked up the unopened envelope and held it out to her. She slowly ran her fingers over Christian's name, obviously penned by Samuel. Hannah gasped. "A letter from Samuel?"

Christian nodded and held up the Bible in his lap. "Samuel left this in the *dawdi haus*. There were two envelopes inside."

Hannah's eyebrows lifted. "Two?"

Christian slid another envelope from between the pages of Samuel's Bible. He held it out to Hannah. "This one is for you."

Hannah surveyed Christian's countenance. Was he worried about the contents of the letter? "When did he write these?" she asked, but realized neither of them would have the answer until after they'd read them.

Christian shrugged.

"Are you going to open yours?"

Christian nodded. "I will read mine first."

He gently slipped his finger under the flap and pulled out a single sheet of lined paper. Silently, his eyes skimmed over the ink on the page. A moment later, he handed the note to Hannah to read.

Dear Christian,

I realize that you probably hate me right now and I can't say I blame you. Please don't throw this letter away until you've read the words. You know I'm not one for writing letters. I just wanted to say a couple of things:

I'm sorry for all the pain I've caused you and Hannah. I never meant to come between the two of you, but somehow that's exactly what has happened. I hope that one day you can find forgiveness in your heart for Hannah and me. Please know that if I could go back and change the past, I'd do it in a heartbeat.

Thank you for your friendship. You are the best friend I've ever known. I wish I'd been a better friend to you.

Sincerely,

Samuel

Tears sprung to Hannah's eyes and she grasped Christian's hand. "This is a blessing, *jah?*"

"*Jah,*" Christian agreed. "We were blessed to know Samuel."

Hannah followed Christian's eyes as they now focused on her unopened letter. Her hand shook slightly as she took the envelope from Christian's outstretched hand. Would the contents bring more sorrow for Christian? She desperately hoped it would not.

She silently read Samuel's final words to her.

My Dear Precious Hannah,

My heart is grieved as I write these words. I fear I have lost Christian, my dearest friend.

Ach, there is so much I want to say but I do not have the time. My thoughts are all jumbled, so I pray you can make sense of this. Christian has asked me to leave, and for his sake, I will do so. I hope you and Christian can work out the rift I've caused between you, but I don't know if that will happen. Right now, you and Christian are talking and I fear it will not go well.

If I leave, I may never see you again so I wanted to share some things that have been on my heart.

First of all, I want you to know that I love you. I've loved you since we were fourteen, even before your first buggy ride with Christian. I've always envied him.

Second, I want you to know that I've forgiven you for our boppli. I know I've already told you, but I wanted to put it on paper so that you don't doubt. I pray you will forgive me for my part in this as well, as I realize I am partially to blame. Had things turned out differently, I'm certain we would be married

with many bopplin by now. But we cannot dwell on past mistakes, we must move forward and look to a hopeful future. I do
not blame you for the way things have turned out. We just have
to trust that somehow God has His hand in this.

And finally, I want you to know that God has forgiven you.
This may seem hard for you to grasp since I know you have not
forgiven yourself. But God is merciful and if we humbly come
to Him, there is NO sin He will not forgive. What you have done
is not unpardonable despite how you may feel.

I know you've heard this before, but perhaps it will mean
more to you now. God loves you. God wants you to trust Him as
your Saviour and allow the blood of Jesus to wash away your
sins. Will you do that, Hannah? If you will, it will bring healing
to your soul like nothing else can. It is the only thing that gives
me peace, even when I've messed things up so badly that I don't
know what my next step will be. I know God will guide me. His
Word says He will not suffer the righteous to be moved. Cling
to Him, Hannah. God loves you like no human being ever can.

I hear Christian's buggy driving away now and it sounds as
if he is not happy. This letter could go on forever, but I must go
now and see how you are doing. Please remember these words.

With all my heart,

Samuel

Hannah looked up at Christian and wiped away her tears.
She hesitantly handed the letter to Christian, then walked to
the restroom to fetch a box of tissues. She lingered a while,
allowing Christian time to read her letter in privacy. Instead

of rejoining him in the living room, she remembered the coffee and snacks she'd prepared and headed toward the kitchen. She knew Christian would appreciate the time alone to process Samuel's words.

As Hannah stirred the fresh cream into her coffee, she felt Christian's presence behind her and his strong arms encircled her waist. His comforting embrace spoke more than words could ever say. Hannah turned around and obliged when Christian's hungry lips met hers. When a knock sounded on the back door, a frustrated groan escaped his lips. After gathering their composure, Christian moved to the door to welcome their unexpected guests.

TWENTY-SIX

*B*ishop Hostettler, Deacon Yoder, Minister Esh, and Minister Fisher removed their hats as they entered the home of Christian and Hannah Glick. Visits such as these were not relished among the leaders, but they felt they were necessary to promote holiness in the church. Today they would be seeking repentance and restoration on behalf of a sister that had gone astray.

Judah Hostettler and Minister Fisher were the only two leaders that had previously been informed of the situation. A visit to Samuel Beachy would have also been required, had he not passed on to Glory. He would now stand before God Himself.

The Glicks offered the leaders a seat at the table, since it provided enough space to accommodate all of them. Without asking, Hannah poured water into glasses for each of the leaders and placed a plate of cookies on the table, then sat down beside her husband.

Minister Fisher immediately reached for a cookie and popped it into his mouth. As he reached for another, he caught the bishop's disapproving gaze and reluctantly brought his hand back to his side. He thought to ask for some milk to go with the cookies, but figured Judah wouldn't approve of that either.

Judah warily eyed Hannah as she tightly clenched her uninjured hand. "We have come to seek the restoration of our sister, Hannah Glick," he informed them. They all nodded in unison.

Christian cast an apologetic look at his wife and stood to leave the room, but stopped at the sound of the bishop's voice.

"You may stay, Christian, as this involves you as well."

Christian nodded thankfully and took a seat.

The bishop began, "Let's pray."

A moment of silent prayer passed, and then heads were lifted in unison as the bishop cleared his voice.

"First of all, I want you to know that this situation has been brought to me privately and I have not betrayed that confidence. As far as I know, only we in this room, along with whomever you have confided in, are privy to this information." He glanced at Hannah and Christian. "It will be up to you to share with whomever you choose."

Christian grasped Hannah's hand beneath the table and smiled reassuringly.

"The Scriptures say we must confess our faults one to another. This is necessary for healing. Sin is confessed to God alone for forgiveness. Hannah, please answer my questions according to the truth, as God is our witness. Please clarify if you wish to."

Hannah nodded.

"Is it true that you have committed the sin of fornication with Samuel Beachy outside the bounds of wedlock?"

Heat rose to Hannah's face. "Before Christian and I were married. *Jah.*"

"Is it also true that a child was conceived?"

Tears pricked Hannah's eyes. "*Jah.*"

"Did you choose to end the child's life at the hands of an abortionist?"

"*Jah.*" Hannah's voice wavered and she felt Christian's grip tightening.

"Do you understand that by choosing to end this child's life, you have circumvented God's will for your life?"

Hannah nodded in silence.

"Did Samuel know you were in the family way?"

"*Nee.* Not at the time. But he knew before the accident."

"And what was his reaction when he found out?"

"He said that he wished I would have told him." Hannah gave Christian an apologetic look. "And that if he'd known, we would have married."

"Did you attempt to hide your sin from the child's father and from your husband?"

Hannah glanced at Christian and he encouraged her to answer. "From everyone, *jah.*"

"Do you realize the Scriptures say, '*Be sure your sin will find you out? And nothing is secret, that shall not be made manifest*'?"

"*Jah.*" Hannah sucked in a breath.

"Is it true that you have lost three children as a consequence of this sin?"

Hannah's lip quivered. "*Jah.*"

"Is it true that you were going to leave your husband and live amongst the *Englisch* with Samuel Beachy prior to his death?"

Hannah hung her head. "*Jah.*" As she sobbed, Christian pulled her close.

The bishop's tone gentled. "Are you aware that the Lord God Heavenly Father offers forgiveness for all these sins and more?"

"*Jah.*"

"And have you sought this forgiveness?"

"*Nee.*"

Minister Fisher's voice spoke from across the table. "Why not?"

"Shush, Jonathan. I'm asking the questions here. You're supposed to be in prayerful meditation." Bishop Hostettler reminded his eager son-in-law.

Christian compressed his lips together to conceal an irrepressible smile.

The bishop continued. "Why have you not sought forgiveness?"

"I'm not worthy," Hannah answered.

"Who is worthy?"

Hannah shrugged.

"No one is worthy. That is why Jesus Christ shed His blood on the cross. He was the only one without sin. The Just died for the unjust. He took the punishment for your sin. Will you accept His forgiveness and His payment for your transgressions, Hannah?"

Tears once again pooled in Hannah's eyes. She felt Christian's comforting hand gently squeeze her shoulder and nodded.

"*Gut.* I have one more request. Your sister Deborah approached me with some information. I'd like the two of you to attend a retreat. It is conducted by the local pregnancy care center and designed for post-abortive couples. I feel this will aid greatly in your healing process." He brought out two brochures and placed them on the table in front of Christian and Hannah. "I'd like you to attend as soon as possible. We will be sure that your farm is cared for while you are gone."

Christian's eyebrows raised as he studied the brochure. "The Healing Garden. This is run by the *Englisch?*"

"*Jah.* I'm afraid the Plain community does not offer anything similar. We don't have as much of a need in our communities as the *Englisch* do, but occasionally there are situations such as yours."

Christian looked to Hannah and she nodded in agreement. "We will go," Christian said.

Hannah spoke up. "What will the People say? Surely they will know that we are gone."

"You are going to visit relatives," the bishop stated.

Both Christian and Hannah looked at each other quizzically, then back at the bishop.

He clarified. "Do we all not have the same Creator? Therefore we are all related." He winked.

On a more serious note, Judah added, "This will be kept strictly confidential. Only the two of you have a right to share, if you choose. A public confession is not required in our church, as in our former Old Order. We do not seek to humiliate you or to give the tongue waggers something to gossip about. Our goal is reconciliation and I believe we have achieved that today." He looked at the other ministers and they all nodded in agreement.

Bishop Hostettler's face brightened. "Now let's enjoy some of these cookies. That is, if Jonathan has left any for the rest of us."

TWENTY-SEVEN

Christian clutched Hannah's hand as they sat side by side in an *Englischer's* van. His eyes scanned the roadway as they traveled at speeds he was uncomfortable with. His stomach did a little flip-flop reminding him of an amusement ride he once endured at Hershey Park. He hoped he wasn't going to be sick. Was Hannah as nervous about this as he was?

He glanced at the bench seat in front of them at one of the other six couples in the vehicle. They were young like he and Hannah, and he guessed they'd probably been through an experience similar to their own. That's why they were all in this van, right?

Hopefully, this weekend would prove to be beneficial for all their sakes, but Christian really wanted help for Hannah. Words could not express how much she meant to him and he cringed every time he realized how close he'd come to losing her. And it had all been his own fault.

As the van slowed, he realized they'd come to the entrance of some sort of campground. Christian smiled. He hadn't been camping since he was about ten years old. His family had only been on vacation a couple of times, aside from visiting relatives in other parts of the state. The time they went camping, Samuel had been allowed to come along. He vividly remembered how he'd fallen into the cold stream they'd been fishing in and Samuel pulled him out. He realized that Samuel had probably saved his life that day. *Oh, how I miss Samuel. I'd give anything to be able to go back and change the past.*

Christian noticed that the van had now stopped in a wooded area and several small log cabins dotted the serene landscape. A large brick building, in which he figured their sessions would be held, stood amidst the cabins. As he stepped out of the van, he took a deep breath and delighted in the fragrant pine scent emanating from the trees. It seemed just being in this spectacular environment helped to ease his tension.

"All right," the driver declared. "I think you all have your cabin assignments. There are still a couple of hours before the first session starts in the main building, so take a little time to rest and settle in. If anybody has any questions, please ask them now."

The counselor looked to each couple. No one spoke up.

"All right, then. We'll see you all at six," he said.

After Hannah and Christian had emptied their extra clothing into the bureau provided, they'd enjoyed a quiet walk around the premises. Since they'd been traveling in the car so long, neither of them felt like resting. Now, it was nearing six o'clock and they headed toward the main building.

Hannah heard a rumble and she smiled at her husband. "Getting hungry already?"

Christian patted his belly. "It seems that way. I wonder how long it will be before we eat dinner."

Hannah shrugged. "I guess we'll find out soon."

She walked through one of the large glass doors Christian held open for her. Noises inside one of the rooms alerted them to where their first session would be held. They walked into the room where two of the couples already sat at tables. A small podium stood at the front of the room, but the speaker was shuffling through some papers atop a counter near one of the walls.

"Go ahead and find a seat at one of the tables," the female speaker informed them. "Two couples per table please. As soon as everyone is present we will begin."

Christian and Hannah joined an older couple at one of the round tables and sat down. Hannah recognized the man's exuberant voice from the van. The gentleman's rotund face brightened and he extended a hand to Christian. "Name's Ronald T, heavy on the T! This is my wife, Judy."

Hannah apprehensively glanced at Christian. This *Englischer* sure was strange. What did he mean by 'heavy on the T?' It didn't make any sense to her, but she enjoyed the fella's outgoing nature.

Judy spoke up. "Oh, don't mind Ron. He always greets everyone that way." She smiled at her boisterous husband.

"So, you folks are Amish, eh?" Ron asked. "Or are you from some other group? Quaker, maybe?"

"*Jah.* We are Amish," Christian answered.

"I always thought the horse and buggy thing was pretty cool. I don't think I'd ever give up my Corvette, though."

"Oh, no. He'd never give up his sports cars," his wife agreed. "Or watching NASCAR."

"What did you good folks say your name was?" Ronald asked.

"I am Christian Glick and my *fraa* is Hannah."

"Well, Chris and Hannah Glick. It sure is nice to meet you folks. I think y'all are the first Amish folks I've met," Ron said.

Hannah smiled. She liked these *Englischers.* They put her mind at ease while she anxiously awaited the beginning of the session. To tell the truth, she didn't really want to be here. She'd rather be at home alone with Christian. Their marriage had begun to heal, but they still had a long way to go.

In spite of herself, she couldn't help but wonder what would have happened if she and Samuel had married and she'd kept the baby. How different would their lives have been? Would Samuel and Christian have mended their friendship eventually? Would Samuel still be alive today? *If that were true, it would mean I'm responsible for the deaths of five innocent people.* The thought shook her to the core.

Maybe Christian would have been better off with someone else as his wife. Was it a betrayal to Christian to think that way? She didn't love Christian any less. As a matter of fact, she admired him. He'd been so kind and supportive once he'd realized his part in this mess she'd made. She desperately needed his strength to support her through this.

"Welcome to The Healing Garden everyone. Let's start with prayer." The speaker's voice captured Hannah's attention and silenced the chatter from the tables. "I hope you're all enjoying your accommodations. Our first session won't be too lengthy because I know you are all starving."

Everyone nodded their heads in agreement and appreciation.

"We'll begin with introductions. I'll start. My name is Beverly Clark and I'm from Philadelphia. My first child, Michael, has been in Heaven twenty years now. Not one day goes by that I don't regret having my abortion." The woman wiped away a tear as did several others in the room. "Know that every person helping out at this retreat has been touched by abortion one way or another. We know what you're going through, so don't hesitate to come to us for anything. You don't need to share your personal story with the group, but you may if you'd like. For now though, just your name will be sufficient. And please tell us what you'd like to get out of this class."

Ron stood up first. "Name's Ronald T, heavy on the T! I'm originally from Cali-forn-i-a, but I've been all over the beautiful U.S. of A. We now live in hairy Harrisburg." The group chuckled. His faced sobered. "I'd like to find closure and be at peace with the past."

After his wife Judy introduced herself, each person took a turn. It turned out that all of them were from the eastern half of Pennsylvania. It seemed as though Hannah and Christian were one of the younger couples in the group. Although half of the attendees appeared to be in their thirties or forties, one couple seemed to be just out of their teen years.

All eyes turned to Beverly when she spoke again. "Jim is going to hand out notebooks to each of you. This is where you'll be completing all of your writing assignments. The first assignment will be to write your story. We all have a story or we wouldn't be here. Perhaps you've never told your whole story to anyone before. We've found that just writing your story down on paper can be tremendously freeing. This is your first step on the road to healing. And don't worry, you won't have to share it with anyone if you don't want to. This is for yourself and for the Lord. Feel free to pour your heart out onto the paper."

After a pleasant dinner with the other couples and the leaders of the retreat, Hannah was anxious to get back to their cabin and begin writing her story. Thankfully, it had been her left arm that broke, otherwise, she wouldn't have been able to complete any of the writing assignments.

She quickly discovered that the counselor had been correct. With each line she wrote, she felt as though one of the shackles had loosened. And by the time her story was entirely written out, one of the links had fallen off. It would still be a long way until she was completely free, but the door had been cracked open and a smidgen of hope broke through the darkness.

TWENTY-EIGHT

As the weekend progressed, Christian and Hannah both felt as though they'd come a long way. They discovered that Post-Abortion Syndrome is wrought by intense trauma and, in order to cope, they had erected certain defense mechanisms. As the symptoms of PAS were read – among them were guilt, fear, flashbacks/nightmares, depression and thoughts of suicide, longing to replace the child that had been lost, along with others – Hannah recognized that she had been experiencing many of them.

Christian also carried around many burdens associated with the abortion, even though the child hadn't been his. He remembered how he'd felt after Hannah had miscarried each of their three, and now sympathized with Samuel. He realized Samuel had probably been reeling from the loss of his child at the time of his death. *Why is that I was so engulfed in my own pain, that I couldn't see Samuel's? And all I had was condemnation for my best friend when he'd needed me most.* The thought grieved his heart mercilessly.

After they had gone through several activities with the other attendees, most of them involving writing, their weekend was quickly coming to a close. The exercises had dealt with relief and denial, anger, and depression. All of these elements were like bricks in a wall that had been erected in their lives. And each one necessitated breaking down prior to forgiveness and healing taking place.

Now, for the toughest part of all: letting go.

"For this final exercise, we'd like each participant to write a letter to your lost loved one. If you've lost more than one child, write a letter to each one," the instructor advised. "And if you haven't given your child a name yet, consider doing that now. We will meet back in this room after lunch. The memorial service will conclude our weekend."

Hannah turned to Christian. "I will write four letters: one for each of our three and one for Samuel's." The hurt that Hannah expected to see in Christian's eyes was non-existent – evidence he'd dealt with his previous anger and guilt. He now only held empathy and understanding.

Christian grasped his wife's hand and squeezed it reassuringly. "*Jah*, I will too."

"I'm so glad you're here with me, Christian. It is difficult, for certain sure, but without you it would be much more so." She leaned into her husband's embrace.

"I love you, Hannah. And I promise I'll never leave you again. I can see now how God put us together. We need each other." Christian paused. "And I don't know if you realize this or not, but I think I needed this just as much as you did."

Hannah wanted to kiss away the tears in Christian's eyes. She was grateful they had both grown so much over these last couple of days, and there was no doubt in Hannah's mind that *Der Herr* had orchestrated it all.

Hannah named her and Samuel's first and only child after its father; and since she didn't know whether the child was male or female, Hannah named the baby Sam – appropriate for either gender.

She and Christian both decided on names for their three lost little ones. Since the first two had been boys, they'd been named Chris, after Christian, and Silas, after Hannah's father. The third child – a girl – was named Miriam, after Hannah's mother.

After Christian and Hannah arrived back at their cabin, Hannah pulled out her notebook and began lovingly penning the words she'd kept bottled up inside for years. The first letter to little Sam seemed to be the most difficult because she'd realized the innocent child had undoubtedly suffered pain during the abortion. She, the mother who was meant to love, protect, and nurture her unborn child, had instead consented to her baby's death. Although she'd tried to forgive herself for that horrifying act, it proved to be a daily struggle.

The ink on the page blurred as the floodgates opened and she poured out her heart to her little one. Admitting her sin to baby Sam on paper had been more difficult than telling the baby's father about it. She knew now that Samuel probably would have given his life for their little one and that realization shamed her.

But she quickly reminded herself that she no longer needed to hold on to her guilt and that Christ's sacrifice was sufficient to forgive her guilt and shame. *My grace is sufficient for thee.* The words soothed her soul like a healing balm.

"This final session usually proves to be the most healing and most memorable for our attendees. We'd like each of you to come up to the podium, one by one or with your spouse, and read the letters to your loved ones. After you've read your letters, place them in the box at the foot of the cross." The speaker gestured toward a rugged two foot wooden cross that sat atop a table with a beautifully carved white box in front of it. "We will bury the box as a representation of our sins being buried with Christ and as a symbol of releasing our loved ones into the Father's hands."

To Christian's surprise, Hannah shot up from her seat first. He grasped her hand. "Do you want me to go with you?"

Hannah shook her head. "I need to do it on my own."

With a strength Christian had never witnessed, he watched as his *fraa* confidently approached the podium. The first three letters she'd read were to their little ones that she'd miscarried and Hannah had read them with a few tears. When she read the last one to Samuel's *boppli,* he was certain there wasn't a dry eye in the room.

Dear Little Sam,

Hello, Sweet One. You may not know me, but I am your Mamm. I look forward to the day we can meet face to face.

First of all, I want to say that I hope you're happy up in Heaven with Jesus. I know it must be beautiful up there. I'm sure you've already met your brothers and sister. And your dat. I bet he was so excited to see you. He loves you very much.

I'm so sorry for ending your life. If there is anything in my life that I could go back and undo, that would be it. I'm sorry that I was selfish and valued myself and my life above yours. I'm sorry that I didn't love and cherish you as a mother should. I'm sorry that I'll never know you this side of Heaven.

Please forgive me.

One day I hope to give you the love that you should have had here. I look forward to the day I can hold you in my arms. If only I could do that now...

I know that I can't, but because of what Jesus did for me, I know I will see you in Heaven one day.

Goodbye, Sweet One!

Mamm

After the final ceremony and burial, every couple was presented with a brass plate for each of their aborted children and a brick for each child that had been miscarried. They were informed that the plaques and bricks could be imprinted with their children's names and sent or taken to the National Memorial for the Unborn in Chattanooga, Tennessee and affixed to the wall of names of lost innocents.

Christian determined that he would take Hannah to Tennessee and have their children's names added to the thousands of others memorialized there.

TWENTY-NINE

*A*lthough the retreat had been refreshing, Hannah was thankful to be home. To her, it seemed as though she and Christian had barely gotten married and they were just beginning their lives together. Now, though, she wasn't hiding any secrets and she could be completely open with Christian. Just that burden being lifted felt so *gut*.

She'd come home from the retreat with a list of things she needed to do. Number one on the list was telling her parents, Samuel's parents, and Christian's parents about the abortion and the impact it'd had on all their lives. It was not going to be an easy task. Hannah now knew the destruction keeping secrets could bring; especially a secret of this magnitude.

Christian leaned over her shoulder from behind the couch and pecked her cheek. "Whatcha doin'?"

"*Ach*, just thinkin' about how our folks and Samuel's folks will react. I'm scared, Christian."

He rounded the couch and abruptly plopped down next to her. He took her hand in his. "Give it to God. Remember, you cannot control others' reactions. Keep in consideration their pain and give them grace. I don't expect them to be happy about it."

"*Nee*, that they will not be. I just wish it wasn't so hard." She brushed away a tear.

"It will get easier. It already has, *jah*?" He squeezed her hand.

"Yes. The retreat helped a lot. *Denki* for everything, Christian. For understanding and helping me through all this. I don't know where I'd be without you."

"It is not me that has carried you through this. It was *Der Herr*." Christian loosened her *kapp* and delightfully watched her long hair tumble down from her bun. "*Kumm*, tomorrow will be a long day. You need your rest."

Hannah took a deep breath as she knocked on the back door of the Beachy home. She and Christian had seen Samuel's father enter the barn just prior to their arrival. Surely he was busy working in his harness shop and didn't wish to be disturbed. Maybe they should come back another time.

Just as Hannah'd convinced herself to turn around, Samuel's mother answered the door. "Hannah, Christian! To what pleasure do we owe this visit?" Her smile welcomed them into the house.

Oh Lord, please help me. "We need to discuss something important with you and your husband," Hannah said as she felt Christian's hand of support on the small of her back. "It is best if the *kinner* are not around."

Her countenance quickly sobered. "Paul is in the barn. How about if we join him there?"

Hannah cringed. The last place she wanted to be was in Samuel's parents' barn. Even though she attempted to suppress them, memories of her intimate time with Samuel still plagued her conscience. She didn't say anything and quietly followed Samuel's mother out to the barn.

"Paul," Samuel's mother called out. "Christian and Hannah are here. They say they have something important to discuss with us."

Samuel's father set the leather strap he'd been working with down on his work table and wiped his hands on a nearby rag. He extended his hand to Christian and nodded politely to Hannah.

Hannah's toes curled inside her shoes. She took a deep breath. "You are not going to like what I have to say, but I must say it anyway." She closed her eyes and swallowed hard, summoning the courage to speak the words she knew she must. "Before Christian and I married, Samuel and I conceived a child. I ended the *boppli*'s life without him knowing."

Hannah watched as the reality slowly set in. She continued. "When he returned from Ohio, just prior to his death, he found out about our *boppli*. He...he was not happy with what I'd done, but he did forgive me. I hope you will too." Hannah handed

Samuel's mother the letter Samuel had written to her. "I'm... I'm so sorry." Hannah wiped a tear from her cheek.

Confusion was replaced with shock which now registered on their expressions. Samuel's mother looked as though all the blood had drained from her face. "You mean our Samuel had a child? I don't believe this." She shook her head. "How...Why...I don't know what to say."

"Surely our son would have informed us if he'd had a child," Paul stated skeptically.

She glanced up at Samuel's father. "Samuel didn't know. He went out to Ohio before I found out that I was in the family way," Hannah explained. "He didn't know until the day he died. He probably would have told you about it eventually."

"Wait, what do you mean you *ended* the child's life?" Samuel's mother asked.

Hannah sucked in a breath. "I had an abortion."

She gasped. Full realization had finally sunk in. "You... you aborted *our grossboppli*? You killed Samuel's only child?" Hannah watched as tears formed in Samuel's mother's eyes. "How could you do that? Who gave *you* the right to play God?"

This is exactly what Hannah was afraid of. "Nobody. I'm sorry."

"We could have a..." she counted on her fingers "...a five-six year old grandchild. He or she would be starting school now."

Tears rose in Hannah's eyes. How many times had she had those very same thoughts? She remained silent. What could she say?

"If you didn't want Samuel's *boppli,* I surely would have taken it. How could you be so selfish, Hannah? To not only hide Samuel's baby from him, but to deny Paul and me the right to our own *grossboppli*? Imagine, Paul, we could be raising Samuel's *boppli* now." She brushed away a tear.

"We will go now," Christian spoke.

"Yes, I think you need to," Paul agreed.

Samuel's mother spoke again. "I must say, I'm ashamed of you, Hannah Glick. I thought you had more decency than that. I never would have thought that sweet little Hannah Stolzfus would become a murderer. The bishop should have you shunned for this. I –"

"That's enough!" Christian's voice rose. "Have you never made a mistake in your life? Why don't you just pick up a stone and throw it at her? Did you not hear her say that she's sorry?"

Christian put his arm around his wife. "Let's go, Hannah." He led her out of the barn to their buggy, opened the door for Hannah, and helped her up. "I'm sorry, Hannah. I did not expect Samuel's parents to react that way."

"Neither did I, but I think I understand. They are hurting. They've recently lost their son and now their grandchild. We must not hold any bitterness against them." Hannah watched the trees passing by as they neared the edge of the Beachy property.

"You're right. I just hope it goes better with our parents," Christian said.

"I don't think it could get any worse, *jah*?"

"I don't see how it could. I admire you, Hannah. You are a strong woman."

She squeezed his hand. "*Denki*, Christian. But I assure you, I do not feel strong."

As Hannah and Christian sat in her parents' living room, her mother gathered her in a comforting embrace.

"I knew something was wrong." Miriam shook her head. "I'm sorry, Hannah. I had no idea you were suffering so much. I wish you would have come to us in the first place. I know we would have been upset at first, but we could have gotten through it. I'm sorry if there was anything I did or said that made you think you couldn't confide in me." Her eyes filled with compassion.

"I was just so scared, *Mamm*. I was afraid that Samuel didn't love me anymore. Scared that you and *Dat* would be disappointed. Afraid of hurting Christian and being rejected. I didn't know what to do. I thought everything would be easier if I just wasn't pregnant. But what I didn't realize is that the abortion did not make me un-pregnant. It made me the mother of a dead baby. If I had any idea how much sorrow it would cause, how much more complicated it would actually make my life..." She shook her head. "I've messed up so many things. We've lost so much because of my decision. Christian and I will never have our own *bopplin*."

"*Jah*, that is true. But *Der Herr* has forgiven you, Hannah," her father Silas reminded.

Hannah swiped the moisture from her eyes. "I know, *Dat*. I just wish I would have been wiser. I wish I would have done things differently."

"We all wish that we could do that; but we can't, can we? It is all in *Gott*'s hands, Hannah," her mother assured. "*Der Herr* can take the disgraceful and turn it into something beautiful. He has already healed your and Christian's marriage, *jah*?"

Hannah glanced at her husband's smiling face. Oh, she was so thankful for his support. "*Jah*. Christian has been wonderful." Christian squeezed her hand.

"Will you stay for dinner?" *Mamm* asked, changing the subject.

Christian looked to Hannah and raised his eyebrows.

"*Ach, denki* for asking, *Mamm*. But we still need to visit Christian's folks tonight," she said regrettably.

"Why don't the two of you come for supper after meeting on Sunday then? How does that sound?" *Mamm* asked.

Christian perked up. "That sounds great. Hannah and I would love to come."

"And we would love to have you," Silas added.

Christian's folks had also responded with empathy and understanding. While they were saddened that they would never have *grossbopplin* from Hannah and Christian and disappoint-ed that Christian would not have an heir to carry on his name, they were proud of how their son supported his *fraa*.

With each visit they'd made, including the visit with Samuel's parents, Hannah felt lighter. It was as though, brick by brick, the stone wall was crumbling. She couldn't remember a time, since before the abortion, that she'd felt this free. God truly was gracious!

THIRTY

The idea had come to her in the middle of the night. Hannah shot up from the bed, grabbed her journal from the nightstand, and hurried downstairs to light the lamp. As she sat on the sofa, she quickly penned all she could remember from her dream.

Christian drowsily clomped down the stairs to find Hannah staring intently at the notebook in front of her, a pencil perched between her teeth. Engrossed in her writing, she obviously hadn't heard him descend the steps. Christian yawned noisily and stretched his arms wide.

"Oh, I'm sorry. Did I wake you?" Hannah glanced up, noticing he still wore his white t-shirt and boxers, then quickly refocused her attention back on her notebook.

"No big deal." He graced her lips with a brief kiss. "I'll make us some coffee."

"*Ach*, that sounds *wunderbaar.*"

Christian plodded to the kitchen and returned a short while later with two mugs of the steaming brew. He joined Hannah, opposite the couch where she sat, and pulled his Bible from the end table. "You must be writing some pretty important stuff. I've hardly seen your eyes move from that paper."

"*Ach*, Christian. I had the most *wunderbaar gut* dream. We were here at our house – you and I – and there were girls here." She smiled.

Christian's eyebrows lowered. "Girls?"

"*Jah.* Young women. And they were all expecting *bopplin* except for one or two of them – they already had babies."

Christian wondered where Hannah was going with this and why she seemed so excited. He nodded for her to go on.

"Don't you see Christian? I think it was from *Der Herr.* I'm thinking maybe he wants us to open our home to young women who choose to keep their babies." Hannah's whole countenance lit up like the *Englischer* houses decorated at Christmastime. "I know I must sound *ab im kopp.* I remember a young *Englisch* couple, maybe sixteen or so, at the clinic. It seemed like the girl wanted to keep her *boppli,* but her beau told her no. He said that he would leave her and that her folks would probably shun her if she kept the baby. But what if she had someplace that she could go, Christian? What if she had a safe place to have her *boppli*?"

What could Christian say to Hannah's sparkling eyes? He hadn't seen her this happy in forever, it seemed. He couldn't burst her bubble by telling her that the leaders probably wouldn't approve. He shrugged. "I guess we could talk to Bishop Hostettler and see what he thinks of it."

She jumped up and threw her arms around Christian. "I knew you'd understand."

"Hannah," Christian warned in a cautionary tone. "Don't get your hopes up too high. The leaders might not approve."

"But what if their being here brings them closer to *Der Herr*? What if they find Jesus here? We'll not only tell them about the love of Christ, but we could show them too."

Christian sucked in a breath. "Are you up to this, Hannah? It wouldn't be difficult seeing these young women have *bopplin*?"

Hannah shook her head adamantly. "Don't you see, Christian? We wouldn't need our own *boppli*. We would get to help others have theirs. We would be surrounded by *bopplin*."

"I don't think that would be the same thing, *Schatzi*," he said sympathetically.

"Oh, I know. But it would be something."

Concern now covered Christian's face. "You're not trying to atone for sins that have already been forgiven; are you, Hannah?" He remembered how at the retreat he'd learned one of the symptoms of PAS was attempting to cover guilt with good works.

"*Nee*. I just want to help people. I want to save lives. Imagine if someone had been there to talk me out of it. We might have a houseful of *bopplin*."

Christian swallowed hard. "If someone had talked you out of it, we probably wouldn't be married, Hannah. You would have married Samuel." Christian couldn't help the bitterness in his voice. It had been something that he'd thought about many times. He'd never said anything, but sometimes Christian felt as though Hannah would have rather married Samuel and had his baby.

Hannah noticed Christian's fallen countenance. "I'm sorry, Christian." Her eyes rimmed with tears. "I don't know how things would have turned out. But I know I don't regret marrying you. I thank *Der Herr* every day for giving me you."

Christian couldn't silence the doubt that clouded his thoughts. "If Samuel were still alive, you'd be with him."

"Christian, stop. Don't do this." Hannah rested her hand on his. "I love you."

His eyes were filled with so much pain. "More than you loved him?"

"Please, Christian. I don't want to argue with you. Don't do this."

"Just say it, Hannah! Just say you loved Samuel more than me."

"Why are you doing this, Christian?" Hannah sobbed.

"Because I want to know the truth."

"I loved both of you."

"If that's true, then why did you give yourself away to Samuel? You barely let me kiss you, Hannah, and you gave yourself – all of you – to Samuel."

"You said you'd forgiven me for that. Why do you keep bringing it up?"

"Because maybe I can't forget about it. Maybe I wonder, every time we share our marriage bed, whether you're thinking of me or him. Maybe I wonder if you'd have been happier with Samuel. You chose him before we were married. And before his death, you'd chosen him again. Why?"

"*You* rejected *me*, Christian. Have you forgotten? You rejected me and Samuel was there. He was there for me when nobody else was – including you." Hannah sighed. "Don't you see, Christian? I've always loved you. *You* were not my second choice, Samuel was. Did I love him? Yes. Do I love you? Yes. Can't you see that it was God's original intention for *us* to be together? I know I made a mess of things. But can we *please* just put all this behind us? I don't want to deal with this anymore. I *can't* deal with this anymore. I need a normal life, Christian. I need you to accept me for who I am and we need to move on. This hurts too much. I don't want hurt anymore," she cried in desperation.

Christian's shoulders dropped at her words and he chided himself. How could he have heaped this burden on her? They'd been doing so well. Hannah had finally found something to be happy about, and he had to crush it. Christian opened his arms and gathered Hannah close. "I'm sorry, Hannah. I'm sorry I brought that up again. Forgive me," he spoke into her hair.

Christian resolved, from that point forward, to never mention the hurtful things of the past again. As much as he could help it, he would only dwell on the positive.

"No."

Hannah hadn't expected the bishop's response to be so concise. "But we could help people. We would be sharing God's love and –"

"I'm really sorry, Hannah. The leaders have unanimously agreed that it would not be in our best interests. I do believe the *Englisch* already have places like that. And we don't want to encourage wantonness amongst our young people," Judah Hostettler said.

Hannah remained silent.

"Perhaps you will consider helping out some other way. I know they need volunteers at the crisis pregnancy centers and some women even stand in front of clinics and try to persuade women not to abort," he suggested.

"I don't know if I would feel comfortable doing those things," Hannah said hesitantly.

Judah patted her arm. "Just pray about it, Hannah. The Lord will direct you."

"*Jah*, I will do that."

As she and Christian traveled home from their meeting with the bishop, Hannah couldn't help but feel defeated. She wanted to do something so badly. If she could just make a difference, just save one life, then she'd feel like she'd accomplished *something*.

Perhaps she would go back to the clinic to speak with some of the young women, although she dreaded the thought of setting eyes on that horrid place again. *Would I have listened to someone? Maybe if someone had offered me hope.* All she could remember is how desperate and hopeless she'd felt. She was almost certain that if someone – anyone – would have offered her an alternative, she may have taken it.

THIRTY-ONE

Two days a week for a month, Hannah had been going to the clinic on Elm Street to try to talk to the young women entering the establishment. If they didn't avoid her altogether, they certainly didn't appear as though they wanted to hear a word she said. Although one or two women had politely listened for a minute or two, she hadn't made a difference.

After the first week, she thought that perhaps she should write a letter about what she'd gone through. Maybe the women would take it into the clinic with them and read it. All she knew is that she felt like a failure. In all her efforts, she hadn't been able to persuade one woman.

"So will you keep going to the clinic?" Deborah asked over her bowl of soup.

Hannah shook her head as she ladled some soup into her own dish. "I don't think I want to. I wish there was something else I could do." She tapped on her notebook, thinking for a moment.

"Wow. You've filled that journal up fast. Is that your second one?" Christian asked.

"Third. I feel like it's my best friend. I write about everything." She laughed.

"I know. You have that thing everywhere you go." Christian scratched his head.

Peter spoke up. "Hey, what about a book?"

Hannah's lips twisted. "A book?"

"*Jah.* Have you thought of writing a book about your life and all that you've been through? I bet that would be a way you could make a difference." He raised his eyebrows.

Hannah's face illuminated. "*Ach*, Peter. I think that's a *wunderbaar* idea!" Hannah hesitated, eyeing Christian. "But...do you think the leaders would approve?"

"I don't see why not," Christian said.

Hannah shot up from the table with her notebook in tow.

"What are you doing?" Christian asked.

"Starting my book." Hannah smiled.

"Now? I didn't mean at this instant," Peter said, feeling a little guilty his suggestion disrupted their dinner.

"I know, but I just got an idea for the introduction and if I don't write it down right away, I might forget it."

"But we just sat down for dinner," Deborah protested.

"I'll be back in a couple of minutes, I promise."

Christian sighed as his *fraa* walked away. "Okay."

Deborah laughed. "When Hannah sets her mind to something, it's not easy to persuade her otherwise."

"Believe me, I know," Christian agreed.

"Sounds a lot like someone else I know," Peter said, winking at his wife.

True to her word, Hannah returned to the table a few moments later. Her notebook was still tucked under her arm.

"Well?" Deb asked.

"Well, what?" Hannah grasped her spoon, delighted that her soup had now cooled enough to enjoy.

"Aren't you going to read it to us?"

Hannah's cheeks flushed. "*Nee.*"

"Why not?" Christian joined the conversation.

"Well, it's just my first thoughts. A draft is all. I might decide to change it," Hannah said.

"May I see it?" Christian asked.

Hannah nodded and sheepishly handed over her notebook.

Christian's eyes skimmed over the page. A smile spread across his face. "Hannah, this is good!"

Hannah never did know how to respond to praise. It had always been frowned upon by their People. "*Denki,*" she whispered timidly.

"Do you mind if I read it?" Deborah asked.

Hannah shrugged. What was the point? It's not like they wouldn't read it eventually.

Deborah received the notebook from Christian's outstretched hand. To Hannah's dismay, she began reading aloud:

"*Hannah's Hope. Introduction: The story that you are about to read is true. It is my story. It has taken me many years to overcome my grief, but by God's grace, it has been over-come. My desire in writing this book is three-fold. One, if you have experienced the pain of abortion, my hope is that you'll find healing. Two, if you are considering abortion as an option, I hope you will seriously consider the consequences first. And three, I pray that you'll find the joy and peace that knowing Jesus Christ can bring..."*

"That is really good, Hannah," Peter agreed. "I think my *bruder* would be proud." He attempted to swallow the emotion in his voice.

Hannah nodded humbly. "*Denki* for saying that, Peter. It means a lot." Hannah glanced at Christian to gauge his reaction. Thankfully, he didn't seem bothered. The last thing she desired was more tension between herself and Christian.

"I like the title. Hannah's Hope," Deborah said wistfully. "This is great. I think you may be able to impact a lot more lives than you think."

"That is my desire," Hannah said.

THIRTY-TWO

Several months later, the completion of Hannah's book seemed more and more like a reality. Writing had become so much easier once her cast had been removed. She still had a way to go, but the majority had already been penned. She hoped that Bishop Hostettler would be willing to formally recommend her book by allowing her to use his quotation on the cover of her book. She was unsure whether he would approve it or not, knowing that he might see it as *hochmut*.

After meeting on Sunday, she approached Judah during the common meal.

"How is the book coming along?" the bishop asked.

"*Ach, gut.* That's what I was wanting to talk to you about. Would you be willing to recommend my book? I mean, after you've read it and approved of it," she said.

"Why don't we cross that bridge when we come to it, *jah*?" Bishop Hostettler rubbed his beard, glancing over Hannah's shoulder. "Is your husband around?"

Hannah scanned the congregants that now gathered around tables, each taking their turn to eat. She quickly spotted Christian sitting near her father and Peter Beachy. It almost seemed as though Peter had stepped in and filled the role Samuel had left vacant in Christian's life. The two had become close friends, to which Hannah was thankful.

"He is sitting near my *vatter*," Hannah said.

"I would like to speak with the two of you privately before you leave today," Judah said.

"Okay, Bishop. I will let Christian know." Hannah wondered what the bishop wished to speak with them about and hoped she hadn't said or done anything to cause trouble. Samuel's folks still seemed to be put off by her, but she didn't feel like there was much she could do about it. She knew that oftentimes hurtful people were hurting people, so she determined to pray for them all the more. Perhaps someday *Der Herr* would bring healing to their lives.

Christian and Hannah sat under the shade of a large poplar tree near the Fishers' home. They waited patiently while Bishop Hostettler sipped on his iced tea. Hannah clenched and unclenched her hands several times, hoping that Judah would just come out and say whatever it was.

"I have a proposition for the two of you," the bishop began. "A friend of mine, also a bishop, out in Indiana has a…situation. Now, mind you, this is confidential information," he warned.

Both Christian and Hannah nodded in understanding.

"His granddaughter is fifteen. And expecting a *boppli*." He sighed. "He asked if she could come to Paradise until the *boppli* is born, then she will return to Indiana. The father of the child is *Englisch* and has refused to take responsibility. She has decided to offer the baby for adoption." He surveyed their hopeful faces. "I informed him that I might know of a couple that would be willing to take the girl in and adopt the *boppli*. Am I correct in my assumption?"

Hannah's countenance irradiated joy as she looked to Christian for approval.

"The *vatter* does not want the child?" Christian was dumbfounded.

"He has already signed papers releasing his interest in the babe," Judah said.

"Are you certain the mother will give the *boppli* up?" Christian asked.

"Only to a *gut* Amish family."

Christian glanced at Hannah and smiled. "When will she come?"

"Next week, if you are ready."

Hannah smiled. "We're ready now."

"*Gut*. I will let him know." Judah nodded in satisfaction.

J. E. B. Spredemann

Hannah and Christian anxiously awaited the arrival of their guests. It had seemed like forever since they'd hoped for a child, and now the dream they thought impossible might become a reality. Hannah knew there were many things that could go wrong, but she chose to dwell on the positive and trust *Der Herr* with the outcome.

The train was due to arrive at two o'clock tomorrow afternoon and Hannah was nearly bursting at the seams. She lay awake tossing and turning. There was no way she'd be getting any sleep tonight.

"Can't sleep, huh?" Christian rolled over on his side to face her. His eyes attempted to adjust to the darkness.

"*Nee.* Christian, I'm so excited."

He laughed. "Yeah, I kinda noticed."

"What do you think our *boppli* will look like?"

"Whoa, there. Don't you think you're gettin' the cart before the horse? We still have several months and you know as well as I do that any number of things could happen between now and then."

"I know, Christian. Trust me, I'm trying to prepare myself for the worst, but I'm choosing to trust God with whatever happens. I know that it's all in His hands."

"Well, I can't help but think that *Der Herr* has His hand in this." Christian reached over and stroked Hannah's hair. He couldn't see her long tresses, but his mind's eye painted a pretty vivid picture.

Hannah yawned, leaning back down into her pillow. "Do you want a boy or a girl?"

Christian shrugged as though she could see him. "At this point, I don't care. Any *boppli* will be a blessing." He leaned closer, nuzzling his *fraa's* neck.

"I agree," Hannah said, yawning again. Her eyelids became heavy in the darkness, but she struggled to keep them pried open.

"How about if…" – Christian continued his romantic intentions – "we leave early tomorrow and go someplace special for lunch?"

No response.

"Hannah?" he whispered. "Hannah?" Christian heard his wife's soft breathing and realized she was asleep. "So much for my attempt at romance," he mumbled. "Next time I'll have to light the lantern."

Christian lay awake for another hour while his *fraa* slept soundly by his side, then he eventually drifted off to dreamland as well.

Hannah stood from the bench on the platform and impatiently walked over to the tracks, craning her neck to listen for any sign of motion.

"Hannah, we're two hours early. Come sit down," Christian urged from his spot on one of the plastic benches.

"I'm tired of sitting," she complained.

"You're just antsy. The train isn't coming until two o'clock and no amount of looking down the tracks is going to make it arrive sooner," he reasoned. "*Kumm*...sit with me, *Lieb*."

Hannah acquiesced at Christian's request.

"Why don't you eat your lunch now? You barely took two bites at the restaurant." He handed her the Styrofoam container full of food.

She sighed. "I'll try."

An hour and forty minutes later, a loud whistle blew down the tracks.

"*Ach*, they're here, Christian!" Hannah squealed, jumping up from the bench.

As the large metal locomotive screeched to a halt, passengers for the next train began lining up on the platform.

There were four different passenger cars, so Hannah kept an eye on two of them while Christian watched the others. Passengers poured out from each doorway. Looking through the windows, Hannah immediately spotted a rounded prayer *kapp*, indicative of some Indiana Amish groups. She rushed over to Christian and pointed out the *kapp* inside the train car.

"That must be her," Christian agreed.

When a petite blonde girl stepped out of the train, Hannah gasped and looked at Christian. "She looks like a child," she whispered, far enough away for only Christian to hear.

The young girl's eyes scanned the platform and she smiled hesitantly when she saw Hannah and Christian approaching her.

"Julia?" Christian asked.

"*Jah.* I'm Julia Graber." The girl's soft blue eyes showed relief. She clutched her bag tightly.

"I am Hannah and this is my husband, Christian." Hannah held out her hand, as likewise did Christian.

She shook both of their hands and one corner of her mouth lifted slightly.

"Well, I bet you're tired," Christian said. "I'll carry your bag. Our driver should be here soon, if he's not waiting already."

She nodded and followed Christian; Hannah walked beside her.

THIRTY-THREE

*J*ulia plopped down onto the bed in the Glick's extra bedroom and closed her eyes. All she felt like doing is sleeping now, but she couldn't fall asleep. The train ride had been a lot longer than she'd anticipated and the constant rocking did not sit well with her stomach. Fortunately, her morning sickness was over for the most part. Only now did she occasionally feel nauseous.

Dawdi had been correct about the Glicks. They seemed like a really nice couple. She wondered why they couldn't have children, but she wouldn't ask. She knew folks that had those kind of troubles usually didn't like to talk about them. She was thankful that her *boppli* would be going to a family that cherished children. Of course, most Amish families that she knew did.

Leighton sure didn't. No, all he wanted from her was one thing – and it didn't include a baby. When they first met he'd been so sweet and caring. She was certain he was a good man, one she could trust. He was three years older than her and he seemed so mature. And he was *Englisch*.

They had been dating for a few months before they began a physical relationship. Julia didn't doubt that she'd loved him, but she knew now that his profession of love had not been sincere. She'd been naïve to believe Leighton's lie that giving herself to him proved her love. No, she could see now that it only proved one thing: his selfishness.

When she'd told him about the baby, he was shocked. As if he didn't know how babies were made. Julia rolled her eyes. Leighton pretended to care for her after he found out about the *boppli*. At least, he did until she refused to keep sleeping with him. Now it was *her* fault that they broke up because she didn't "love" him anymore.

Julia wiped away a tear. Why did Leighton have to end up being a jerk? She actually loved him, wanted to spend the rest of her life with him. But now that she saw his true colors, Julia was glad that he broke up with her. She wouldn't want to be married to someone who didn't value children.

She'd wanted to keep the baby at first, but *Dawdi, Dat, and Mamm* convinced her that giving the *boppli* up would be best. They thought she was too young for the responsibility. Too young? Had she not helped raise her brothers and sisters? She already knew what it was like to have a *boppli*. Would it be so bad?

She was certain that the *boppli* was not the main problem. It was finding a young man to marry her after she'd have the *boppli*. That was why her folks were so concerned. She couldn't blame them. How many Amish folks wanted their sons to marry a girl that had been with another man – one she was not married to? Not a one that she could think of.

So she eventually agreed to give the baby up. And now that she knew the *boppli* would be going to a family that truly wanted a child, she felt like her sacrifice was worthy.

Hannah finally finished it. The book was complete. Now she just needed to have Christian, Deborah, *Mamm*, and Bishop Hostettler read it over. And then of course she needed to proofread it again and probably make a bunch of changes. How long would it be before she could hold the book in her hand?

She set her notebook down and removed her journal from the bureau. She hoped Julia would like it here. When she and Christian settled in for the night, they'd discussed their new guest. The girl had barely said a few words at suppertime. She hoped she was just tired from the trip and not afraid of them.

Hannah wanted Julia to feel as though she were one of the family. Perhaps she could be a mentor to the girl since it seemed they might have a lot in common. Of course, Hannah didn't really know all that much about Julia except that she was a young Amish girl carrying an *Englisch* man's child. Hopefully, they'd get to know each other better as time went on.

One thing was for sure: she had no stones to throw. But just because she'd had to learn some things the hard way didn't mean she couldn't give advice. The counselor at the retreat had encouraged each of them to use their personal tragedy for God's glory, and Hannah aimed to do just that.

Der Herr had even given her a parable. It had come to mind when she and Christian had been walking on a private trail near their cabin at the retreat. The walking trail was absolutely gorgeous with wild herbs and plants of all kinds. Hannah had even recognized some of the herbs as medicinal. She knew several of them were used by Danika Yoder to heal certain ailments or to provide nutrition. And some of the flowers and plants on the trail she'd seen in vases at the grocery store.

But nearby they'd seen a large metal lid that had the word 'sewer' stamped on it and a foul smell emanated from the ground. It was then she realized that the reason the trail was lush and healthy was *because* the sewer was nearby. It amazed her how something so lovely could come from something so offensive.

Isn't that the way God works? She'd thought. He takes the things in our lives that are ugly, disgusting, and downright wicked, and transforms them into something magnificent. Just as the herbs can be used to nourish and heal after they've been fertilized, so can we find healing through God's mercy.

The whole picture reminded her of the quilt *Mamm* had given her and Christian as a wedding gift. *Mamm* had lovingly used the scraps of clothing from her and Christian's childhood outfits and transformed them into something beautiful. But she realized that *Mamm* had left out the torn, soiled, and stained pieces.

But *Der Herr* uses all of our circumstances – even the stained ones. He cleanses them with His precious blood, and makes them not only usable, but lovely as well.

Hannah hoped she could share these wonderful truths with Julia, and perhaps bring healing in her life as well.

Julia opened the door to her room and realized it was already light outside. *Oh no. I hope they don't think I'm slothful.* She hadn't fallen asleep until late and the little rest she did acquire had been fitful. Hurrying down the steps, she noticed Hannah putting the clean dishes away in the cupboard.

"I can help with that," Julia offered.

Hannah turned around with a smile. "Oh *gut*, you are up. No, I don't need any help just now, but I might take you up on that offer when I make bread later." She reached up and placed the last glass on the shelf. "I bet you're hungry."

Julia rubbed her belly. "A little."

"*Gut* because I made a lot more oatmeal this morning than Christian and I could eat. Would you like toast and a banana to go with it?"

"*Jah*, just one slice, though. I can make it if you want me to."

Hannah handed Julia a banana. "*Nee.* I 'spect you probably didn't sleep too *gut*. You look tired."

"I didn't. Guess it's just too much excitement." She wiped the corner of her eye.

"So, how long do you have? For the *boppli*, I mean."

Julia peeled the banana. "About four more months. *Mamm* and *Dat* wanted me to stay home as long as possible, so folks don't ask questions. But I'm startin' to show a bit now, and my dress doesn't hide it anymore."

Hannah turned from the stove and nodded. She set the bowl of oatmeal and toast on the table in front of Julia and removed butter and jam from the refrigerator.

Julia's eyes stared into her bowl of oatmeal. "I know what you must think. That I'm not a very *gut* girl."

"*Ach, nee.* I don't think that at all. Julia, we all make mistakes. I've made plenty," Hannah insisted.

Yeah right. Like what? You burnt your husband's toast one day? Julia didn't speak her thoughts, but instead bit into her banana.

"I did love Leighton, the baby's father," she blabbed. "He was *Englisch*. He said he didn't want the baby, so here I am." She took the knife and buttered her toast. "I guess I should have listened to all those warnings about the *Englisch*. I know we're not supposed to be unequally yoked."

Hannah shrugged. "The *Englisch* aren't so bad, most of them. They just live differently than we do. It's important to have a husband that lives and believes the same way you do. Otherwise, you're asking for problems."

Julia laughed. "Do I know that now! If I had any idea that Leighton would just leave me like that, I never would have gone out with him. Why do boys act all sweet and caring one minute and then just dump you the next? I don't get it."

"How did you meet him?" Hannah changed the subject.

"*Ach*, my friend Nellie and I were at the ice cream shop one day. It was crowded and there were no empty seats when Leighton and his *Englisch* friend walked in. They noticed two empty chairs at our table and asked if they could sit down. We didn't want to be rude, so we let them. We talked for about an hour after finishing our ice cream. I really liked Leighton a lot." Julia smiled and her blue eyes sparkled. "He was handsome and funny and he just seemed really sweet. When he asked if he could see me again, I said yes."

"How long have you known him?" Hannah asked.

"I met him about a year ago. I was still fourteen then, but I think he thought I was older. When my birthday rolled around and he realized I was turning fifteen, he seemed surprised. But I guess he figured three and a half years isn't that big of a difference." She took a bite of her toast and Hannah waited for her to continue. "As soon as he found out about the *boppli* that was pretty much it." She frowned. "Of course, my folks had no idea about Leighton."

"I'm sorry to hear that. I couldn't imagine expectin' a *boppli* being so young." She remembered how frightened she'd been at eighteen.

"Well, I don't have to imagine it. This little one doesn't let me forget." Julia rubbed her belly.

"*Jah*, I guess they do at that age. None of ours lived that long." Hannah frowned.

"How many did ya have?"

"Four."

"I'm sorry. That must've been hard." Julia shook her head.

"*Jah*, 'twas. Very hard." Hannah wiped away a tear.

THIRTY-FOUR

*H*annah and Christian enjoyed Julia's company immensely and they could hardly believe three and half months had already gone by. They were ecstatic about the *boppli*'s upcoming arrival, but they'd be sad to see Julia go. She seemed like part of their family now.

"Oh!" Julia placed a palm behind her back.

"Is it the *boppli*?" Christian set his Bible down and his eyebrows shot up.

Julia exhaled, leaning back into the sofa. "I think it was just another pain. I don't think I'm in labor. Chloe said aches and pains are normal this close to birth."

"Are you sure?" Hannah's brow creased.

"*Jah*. I think I'm fine. But if they keep coming I'll let you know." Julia sipped on her hot tea. "Hannah, I wanted to ask you about something."

"*Jah*?"

"I was wondering if I could have your doll," Julia asked.

"My doll?" Hannah's curiosity rose. What could she be talking about? "I don't know which doll you speak of."

"*Kumm*," Julia invited, walking toward the stairs. "I'll show you."

Hannah shrugged to Christian and followed Julia up the stairs.

When Julia entered the bedroom, she walked over to the nightstand and opened the bottom drawer. She pulled out a small hay doll. "This one," she said, smiling. "It has your name on the back so I figured it must be yours. I think it's cute. I've never seen one like this before. Where is it from?"

How did that get in here? Hannah's eyes widened, and then filled with tears. "Samuel," she whispered.

"Samuel? Who is Samuel?"

"He was the *vatter* of my first *boppli*," Hannah stated.

Julia's mouth hung open. "What? Really? I didn't know you were married to someone before Christian."

"I wasn't."

"You mean…so…you were in the family way? What happened? I mean, why didn't you marry Samuel? Was he *Englisch* too?"

Hannah sighed. She hadn't wanted to bring up anything negative while Julia was here. She really hadn't planned to tell Julia about this, but apparently now it seemed inevitable. "*Nee.* Samuel did not know about our *boppli*. He moved to Ohio to marry someone else. I had an abortion." Hannah hung her head.

Julia's eyes widened. "What? An abor – I don't believe this." Her face twisted with emotion. "I'm not giving my precious *boppli* to someone that has aborted their own child. How could...I – I need to go now." She turned her back to Hannah and began quickly removing her things from the drawers and wall pegs. She sniffled. "Please tell Christian I need a ride to Bishop Hostettler's."

Hannah stood dumbfounded. "But Julia, I –"

"Please just go, Hannah. There's no way you're getting my *boppli* and nothing you say is going to make me change my mind," she said angrily.

Hannah rushed down the stairs and saw Christian standing near his chair.

"I heard Julia raising her voice. What was that all about?"

Hannah burst into tears and fell into Christian's arms. "Oh Christian! She doesn't want us to have the *boppli* anymore. I told her about Baby Sam."

"Shh..." Christian stroked her hair, kissing the top of her head. "It's okay, Hannah. We are trusting *Der Herr*, remember?"

Hannah sobbed, unable to control her tears. "She wants to go to the Hostettlers'."

"I will take her," Christian said. "Why don't you go lay down? It's been a long day, *Lieb*. Pray and trust *Der Herr*, Hannah. He knows best."

It had been a week now since Julia left the Glicks' home. Hannah attempted to stay positive, especially in Christian's presence, but she couldn't help the tears that sometimes came. Trusting *Gott* should be easy by now, nevertheless, that wasn't always the case. She'd been so hopeful when Julia first arrived. Perhaps it wasn't God's will for them to have a child after all. Hannah realized she would be okay with that, but it still hurt.

A honking noise drew Hannah's attention outside. She glanced out the window and noticed a large brown shipping truck. *My book!* Hannah smiled. Her book had finally arrived. She rushed outside, noticing Christian had also come in from the fields.

Christian raised his eyebrows and smiled at Hannah. The delivery man carried a large box from the back of the truck and Christian quickly relieved him of his burden.

"This is for Hannah Glick," the man said.

"*Jah.* That is me," Hannah said.

The man held out an electronic clipboard. "I'll just need you to sign right here."

Hannah signed the digital document, then hastily followed Christian inside the house as the delivery truck drove away. Christian pulled out his pocket knife and carefully opened the box. Hannah reached in and pulled out one of the books. She slowly ran her fingers over the cover and smiled at Christian.

"Hannah's Hope." She read the cover. "Can you believe it, Christian?"

"Scarcely, but *jah*, I can believe it." He put an arm around Hannah and kissed her cheek. "So, you want to go deliver some copies?"

Hannah squealed. "Yes."

"Okay, Deb." Hannah held her book behind her back excitedly. "Close your eyes and hold out your hands."

"Hurry Hannah! You know I can't stand waiting for surprises." She closed her eyes and tapped her foot, her lips curved up in a smile.

"Are your eyes closed all the way?" Hannah waved her hand in front of Deborah's face to make sure.

"*Ach*, Hannah. You know I don't peek anymore."

"Hmm…I'm not so sure about that," Hannah teased.

"Just give it to me…whatever it is!" Deb laughed.

"Okay, okay." Hannah gingerly set the book in Deborah's hands, gauging her reaction.

Deborah's eyes stayed shut as she realized what she was holding. She screamed. "Your book! It's your book." She opened her eyes to prove her assessment.

Hannah smiled as she watched her sister's eyes scrutinize every inch of the paperback.

"*Ach*, Hannah, it's *schee*. I love it." She leaned over and firmly embraced her sister. "I'm so proud of you."

The sentiment brought tears to Hannah's eyes. "It wasn't easy."

"I know it wasn't, *Schweschder*. That's why I'm so proud of you." She released her hold and surveyed her kitchen. She spotted a pen near the letter holder on the wall and quickly retrieved it. "All right, you need to sign it."

"*Ach*, but that's *hochmut*."

"Oh, stop. It's not prideful at all. As a matter of fact, I bet Bishop Hostettler will ask you to sign his too," she teased.

Hannah laughed. "He will not."

Hannah didn't want to personally deliver Bishop Hostettler's copy of her book for fear that Julia would not want to see her, so she waited in the buggy while Christian delivered it. Judah walked out to the buggy with Christian a short while after Hannah had seen her husband enter the bishop's home. Judah's face showed concern and he lifted a half-smile of encouragement. He held up the book. "This is a *gut* thing you have done, Hannah. I pray *Der Herr* will use this for His glory."

"Me, too, Bishop Hostettler," she said meekly.

His eyebrows lifted and his weathered face brightened. "Would you mind signing my book?"

THIRTY-FIVE

*C*hristian stomped his boots on the back steps before opening the door to the kitchen. He'd just listened to the messages on the answering machine in the barn and he was certain the news he had would brighten Hannah's day.

Hannah walked into the kitchen with a pile of folded dish towels in her arms. "What are you so happy about?"

"I just listened to the messages in the barn," he said cryptically.

"Oh yeah?" Hannah pretended to ignore his enthusiasm. She nonchalantly opened the cupboard and slowly placed the towels on the shelf, waiting for Christian's announcement of whatever he seemed so excited about.

"Well, don't you want to know?"

"Only if you want to tell me, Christian."

Christian placed his index finger over his lips and tapped them. "Hmm...do I want to tell you that your book sold five hundred copies?" He shrugged.

Hannah accidentally slammed the cupboard closed in her excitement. "Really? Five hundred copies in one week?" she squealed.

"Mm-hmm."

"*Ach*, Christian, that's *wunderbaar*." She smiled.

"I know. I think we need to celebrate somehow," he agreed, kissing her smiling lips.

"I just made some applesauce cake. We can have it with coffee." She returned his sweet kisses.

"Okay, we can do that," he said. "What are we going to do with all the extra money that comes in from your book sales?" Christian took his seat at the table.

Hannah put some water in the kettle for coffee, then sat across from Christian. "I had an idea about that. How would you feel if we give some to Julia? For the baby, I mean. They'll be going back to Indiana soon."

Christian looked at Hannah and shook his head. "You are an amazing woman, Hannah Glick. How is it that I'm so fortunate?"

"*Nee*, I'm the one that's blessed to have you, Christian." Hannah reached for his hands across the table.

"Do you hear that?" Christian's head perked up. "I think someone's knocking on the front door. It must be an *Englischer*."

"I'll get it," Hannah volunteered.

She walked to the front door and pulled it open. Nobody was there. "Christian, I think you must be hearing things," she hollered back.

Hannah began closing the door when she heard a sound, then she quickly opened it again. She looked at the front porch where she thought she'd heard the noise. "Oh my. Christian, come!" Hannah rushed over to what looked like a mound of blankets and lifted the top layer to peer inside. *A baby? Is this Julia's* boppli?

Christian quickly joined her on the porch. He watched as Hannah lifted the tiny infant and held him in her arms. She pulled the blanket securely around him to keep the chill out. "Look, Christian. An envelope."

He reached into the baby carrier and hastily opened the envelope. He read the words aloud:

Dear Hannah,

I hope you and Christian will keep my boppli. His name is Samuel Christian.

I'm sorry for judging you. Please forgive me. When I read your book, it all made sense. I'm sorry for all you and Christian have lost, but I am glad that you've written a book to help others. It has already helped me. By the way, I took Bishop Hostettler's copy so you might need to give him another one.

I can't think of anybody else I'd rather give my boppli *to. Thank you for all you've done.*

And if Samuel ever asks, please let him know that his mother loved him very much. Please take good care of him.

With Love,

Julia

P.S. Bishop Hostettler has the papers you need to sign.

Christian's eyes glistened as he lifted them to Hannah's. He'd never seen such joy in her eyes as she gazed on their new *boppli.*

A figure appeared around the corner of the house and Christian realized it was Julia. She walked to the steps of the porch. "I just wanted to say goodbye. My driver will be here any minute."

Hannah handed the baby to Christian and abruptly embraced Julia. "*Denki*, Julia. You'll never know how much this means," Hannah said. "Wait here just a minute." Hannah flew into the house and emerged a moment later with the hay doll in her hand. "I want you to have this."

"*Denki.* I'll never forget the two of you and your kindness to me." Julia gave Christian an awkward hug and walked toward her now-waiting vehicle. She waved to them with tears in her eyes as the car pulled away.

Many years later...

Samuel knocked on the door, then stepped into the *dawdi haus* with another gentleman at his side. "*Mamm*, there's someone here to see you."

"Mrs. Glick. Uh...hello. You don't know me but my mother said that she met you about thirty years ago. Her name was Stella," said an unfamiliar *Englisch* man with dark wavy hair and hazel eyes.

Samuel stepped out of the room to give his mother privacy. "Let me know if you need anything."

"*Denki, Sohn.* I will."

"And don't forget, *Mamm*. Ellen and I want you and *Dat* to join us and the *kinner* for supper tonight," Samuel reminded, peeping his head around the doorway before finally leaving.

Hannah nodded and then turned her attention back to her visitor. "You said her name was Stella?"

The *Englischer* nodded.

She wracked her brain attempting to recall a Stella that she had met in the past, but her memory failed her. "I'm sorry, I don't recall your mother."

"That's all right, I understand. From what I heard, she only spoke with you briefly. Anyway, the reason I came is to tell you that your labor has not been in vain. You see, I have been a missionary for about twelve years now. I've been to many countries in Africa, South America, and even to some Middle Eastern countries. I have helped to start many dozens of churches and have personally seen thousands of sinners come to the Lord. And all of that would have never been possible if my mother did not talk to you that day. You see, she was planning to go to the clinic to abort me the day she met you. When you shared your story with her, she knew that God was speaking to her, pleading for my life. She decided to choose life for me and eternal life for herself. So, I'd just like to say thank you on behalf of myself and the others who have turned to Christ as a result of your faithfulness."

Hannah looked into the man's eyes with appreciation and squeezed his strong hand with her aging one. "*Denki*. Thank you so much for sharing that with me. You don't know how much it means."

The man nodded his response before his phone rang. "I'm sorry, I have to go. I have a plane to catch. It has been a blessing to be able to meet you. Thank you for your time, Mrs. Glick." He slipped out the door and Hannah could hear his waning telephone conversation as he walked back to his vehicle.

Hannah looked up toward the sky and closed her eyes. "*Denki, Gott,*" she whispered. "You have been so good to me."

Hannah sat in the Fisher residence, sipping on a glass of freshly-squeezed lemonade. "But Minister Fisher, I don't understand. I know it is not a good thing that I aborted my *boppli*, but it seems as though all these things would not have happened if I hadn't."

"Hannah, God is not willing that any should perish. It was not His will that your child died. What you have been given is a wonderful gift: God's grace. God has shown us that he can take even the worst circumstance and use it for His glory. God's will would have been accomplished in those souls that were saved, with or without you. The miraculous thing is that God gave *you* the privilege to be a part of it."

Hannah suddenly remembered the parable God had given her many years ago and it all made sense. As tears streamed

down Hannah's weathered face, she praised God for His goodness and His unending amazing grace.

EPILOGUE

We'd been down a rough road, Christian and I. But I realized that with every rock we'd hit and every trial that came, we had been strengthened and brought closer to each other and to *Gott*. We've since learned to thank *Der Herr* even in the tough times – especially in the tough times, for it is He that keeps us strong. And I now know that there is *nothing* unforgivable and there are no secrets before an all-knowing merciful God.

*"And we know that all things work together
for good to them that love God, to them who
are the called according to his purpose."*

Romans 8:28

A Letter from the Author

Dear Reader,

I hope you enjoyed Hannah's story. If you're like me, you cried many a tear as you read through the pages. My desire was not to make you cry, but if you did, I know that the story touched your heart in some way.

In researching this book, I've personally learned many things. Namely, that abortion does in fact happen in the Amish community. I'm unsure of the actual statistics for the Amish, but within the Christian church one out of six have experienced abortion. In the unchurched, it is one in three. Wow! How many lives have been lost, how many hurting men and women suffer in the name of choice?

Can you relate to Hannah's story? Has there ever been a time in your life when you thought that it couldn't get any worse – and then it did? Maybe you haven't experienced the pain of abortion, or maybe you have. Whatever you've been through, know that God has been there all along. Many times, I think He just patiently waits for us to cast our cares upon Him.

Have you had to use Plan B? By that, I mean, did you miss out on God's perfect will (Plan A) for your life? Many of us have, probably most. As human beings, we become impatient and tend to take matters into our own hands. It can be difficult to wait on the Lord.

I'm so glad that God promises to never leave us nor forsake us. I'm thankful for Plan B and I sometimes wonder how many times I've missed out on God's perfect will for my life by doing things my own way, or by just plain ignorance. How many blessings did I forfeit, how many eternal rewards have I lost? We can dwell on the negative or we can, like Hannah, move on and let God salvage what's left.

But thankfully, God is more than just a salvager. He is a blessed redeemer. God not only forgives, He restores. God not only heals, He blesses. We see this many times throughout the pages of the Bible. Over and over again, God demonstrates His mercy, compassion, and loving kindness toward His creation. The ultimate manifestation was when Jesus Christ died on the cross and took the penalty for our sins. His redemption is ours for the taking, all we must do is ask and believe. (Romans 10:9-10 KJV)

Like Hannah's sister Deborah, I think most of us are oblivious to the pain others are suffering. I know I am often guilty of being self-centered and unaware of others' needs. How many times have I failed to show compassion to someone who was struggling? Of course, God doesn't expect us to be mind readers but we should be sensitive to those around us. Often times, when we bless others, we ourselves are consequentially blessed as well.

My prayer is that you did not find condemnation, but hope between the pages of this book. I hope you have learned something that you can use, but more importantly, that this book will draw you closer to God and His infallible Word.

Thank you for sharing in Hannah's journey.

To God alone be the glory!

J. Spredemann

A sneak peek at Book 2 in
the Amish Secrets *series…*

A Secret

J.E.B. Spredemann

PROLOGUE

Joseph Bender hung his head, contemplating the implications of his actions. *Am I really shunned?* By the disappointed countenances of his family, he realized it to be true. What would he do now? Where would he go? His father's words played in his mind for the umpteenth time, "You are no longer my son. Leave at once. There is no room in this home for unrepentant sinners."

Joseph heaved a sigh of defeat. He searched his mother's face for some trace of compassion, but she could only look away as she blinked at the tears that trailed her weathered appearance. So desperately he wanted to reach his arms around his mother and embrace her one last time, but he knew the time for affection had passed. It expired the moment Bishop Burkholder read his sentence.

He threw an old duffel bag over his shoulder. It contained the few belongings he owned: two pairs of trousers, two long sleeve cotton shirts, a few undergarments, and socks. He donned his black coat that had seen better days and his straw hat, and walked out of his folks' home, and out of their lives, forever.

In just a few short months, he'd lost everything he'd ever held dear...

Amish Secrets - Book 2

A Secret

Encounter

J.E.B. Spredemann

A Secret Encounter coming December 2013
to participating online retailers

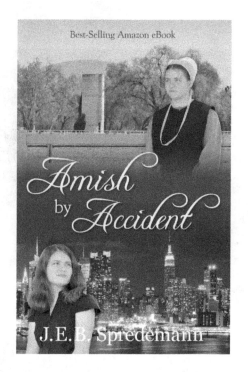

*L*uke Beiler has loved Elisabeth Schrock for as long as he can remember and is looking forward to the day they both join their Amish church so they can marry. Elisabeth, however, chafes under the church rules and flees to the Englisch world leaving Luke heart broken. When an accident leaves Brianna Mitchell with amnesia, she feels helplessly lost. What will happen when she is mistaken for Elisabeth Schrock and taken home to Paradise, Pennsylvania?

Inspirational Christian Fiction

**Amish by Accident available NOW in
eBook, paperback, and audio book**

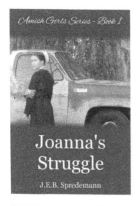

Amish Girls Series - Book 1

Joanna's
Struggle

J.E.B. Spredemann

Amish Girls Series - Book 2

Danika's
Journey

J.E.B. Spredemann

Amish Girls Series - Book 3

Chloe's
Revelation

J.E.B. Spredemann

Amish Girls Series - Book 4

Susanna's
Surprise

J.E.B. Spredemann

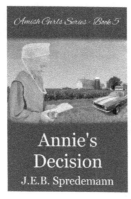

Amish Girls Series - Book 5

Annie's
Decision

J.E.B. Spredemann

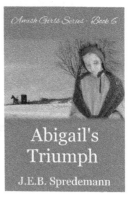

Amish Girls Series - Book 6

Abigail's
Triumph

J.E.B. Spredemann

The Amish Girls Series for teens (eight books in all) is the foundation on which our Christian adult novellas are based. Although all the books (other than Saul's Story) are stand alone, we hope you will enjoy the entire series. May your heart be blessed as you read each character's story of faith, love, friendship, and family.

Amish Girls Series for teens books 1-5 available NOW at participating online retailers

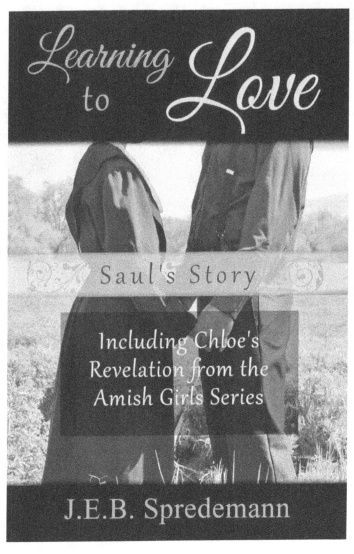

Learning to Love – Saul's Story is a
continuation of Chloe's Revelation

Two Novellas in One (for adults) Coming Spring
2014 at participating online retailers

www.ingramcontent.com/pod-product-compliance
Lightning Source LLC
Chambersburg PA
CBHW021050020225
21280CB00002B/82